the beauty of this street love 2

A TEXAS TALE

ELLE KAYSON

contents

synopsis

The Kinseys. Four brothers and one-up-and-coming sister. They got the street game on lock, but when it comes to the game of love, things ain't so easy.

Tre, the oldest, has his work cut out for him, trying to win back his baby mama, Shamar and cut ties with his ex. Shamar is determined not to settle and if Tre can't step up, she is going to step out.

Tripp is on the verge of losing the family that he and Cyn had just started to build. Cyn's mind is wary of his lifestyle, but her heart craves his love. Can they work it out before their new foundation begins to crumble?

Tamir has a love-hate relationship with Chantal Dubois. Both of them feel betrayed by the other m, and resentment and tension threaten to destroy their love. If they can't overcome past wrongs, their hopes for the future are in vain.

Tyrese, the ultimate player, has always laughed at his brothers' love troubles. But he may have just met his match in Dr.

B. Elyse Rose. He's shocked-- and intrigued--when the good doctor refuses to play the game his way. Can this bad boy convince his "Fairytale Girl" that he's just what she needs.

Baby girl Tamar doesn't know quite what has hit her when she meets Angel Cruz. Dark and mysterious, he sets her passion aflame. But Tamar has some unexpected surprises in store...

Watch as the war with the Prince family heats up and the Kinseys face losing what they've worked so hard to gain and whom they love most!

I swear "The Weekend from Hell" had a new meaning for me. Was it enough that I caught my so-called boyfriend at a damned carwash getting the Superhead treatment? No? How about the fact that this occurred only a few hours after I found out his trifling ass had knocked me up? Not enough? Ok, then. What about the fact that he and his brothers almost killed my godbaby and I had spent the night holding her mother in my arms as she cried her eyes out? *Poor Cyn.*

Is that enough?

I sighed and rolled my eyes heavenward as I let the water from the shower beat down on my tired body. I wanted to pray but I didn't even know what to ask God for. I hadn't imagined bringing a baby into the world like this, but I didn't want to make up with Tremell's ho-ish ass, either. Three days ago, on Friday, you couldn't have told me this would be the sad state of my life.

I rubbed down in body oil, rinsed off, and did a half-ass job at drying off before applying lotion. My mind was whirling and I couldn't reach a decision about anything. I'd usually call Cyn for shit like this, but my boo was broken right now. Devyn and I planned to go check on her later in the afternoon. I couldn't talk to Devyn, even though he was my best friend, too. Dev was like an overprotective brother. He'd tell me Tremell wasn't worth my time and offer to beat his ass. I was kinda happy he punched Tremell Saturday, but I knew in a drawn-out situation, Tremell would kill Dev without a second thought. The only concession he might make would be doing it quickly because he knew I loved Dev. Times like this, I missed my granny and my step-mama, Lora. I wish I had a mother. Mine was so trifling, I had her blocked.

I walked into the kitchen, dressed in my bathrobe, with my hair pulled up into a messy bun near the back of my head. I didn't give a damn about how I looked. My only plans for the day were surviving and making sure my bestie was, too. I felt like kicking my brother Tavi's ass for ever getting us involved with them damned Kinseys. I took my Talenti Sea Salt Caramel gelato from the freezer, grabbed a spoon, and dragged my ass to the living room to plop on a couch. Flipping through the channels, I found one of those messy ass talk shows where people are invited to make fools of themselves. Just what I needed—mindless TV. I dug into the gelato and stared at the screen.

I didn't even look up as I heard the key turn in the lock. There were only two people with keys that Ced and Austin, the men who watched my house, would allow this close without warning. Since I knew Cyn was out of it, that left my sorry ass baby daddy. I laughed at myself as I scraped the sides of the container. I needed to be on one of these damned shows. *"Let's meet Shamar and her 'sorry-ass baby-daddy'."* That's how Jerry Springer would introduce me, right?

He turned off the alarm and started walking towards me.

"You not finna just be coming and going out my house like you please. I need my key," I said, not once taking my eyes off the screen.

"The fuck you talking to, Mouse?"

That earned him a glare. "I'm talking to your grimy ass, Tremell. Give me my key!" I held out my hand. He ignored it

2

and sat down next to me. *Do not acknowledge how good he looks and smells*, I told my stupid brain. Nope, I totally refused to see how delicious he was in his jeans and royal blue tee with a fitted cap sporting the Canadian maple leaf—he'd told me what team that stood for before, but hell if I could remember, especially while he was looking like that.

"Why you got that robe on? You better been in the shower. I been reading and you don't need to be sitting in a whole bunch of hot water. I know your ass loves a bubble bath!" he scolded.

I turned the TV up louder.

"Is that what you're having for lunch? Hell, naw, shorty. That ain't gone feed my baby. You need to be eating right and taking them damned vitamins I had Ced bring you-"

"You got Ced acting like he my daddy just cuz he's older and you acting like you a pregnancy expert now? Leave me alone," I said, slamming down my gelato on the coffee table and moving to stand up. He grabbed my wrist, holding me down to the couch.

"First of all, Ced does that on his own. He been driving and handling business for Pops forever, so he fam. He said you remind him of his daughter that he really didn't get to see. Bitter baby mama drama. Second, you can stay mad as long as you want. But *my* baby ain't gone catch the effects." That pissed me off.

"Ain't nobody *that* gone over your ass! I'm taking care of myself and *my* baby," I said, jerking away from him.

"Shamar-"

"Leave me alone!" I repeated, mugging him.

"You know that ain't about to happen." He moved quickly, pulling my legs up on the couch and settling between them, so that we lay chest to chest. He smiled and ground against me when he realized I was naked beneath the robe. The feel of his denim-covered dick rubbing against my clit had my eyes rolling up in my head. My head fell backwards as he started sucking the sensitive skin of my neck.

"Your little freaky ass," he whispered. "Let's just fuck and make up. Mouse. I don't give a fuck about that girl. She set me up."

It was sooo tempting, especially when his body was over mine, so hard and warm, and the scent of his Creed cologne was tantalizing my nose.

But a part of my mind was chanting, "*I'm not going to be her. I'm not going to be her.*"

"You not gone be who?" His voice snapped me out of my head. Had I said that aloud?

"What?" I asked pushing against him, trying to play it off. To my surprise, he sat up without a struggle.

"Tell me who you not gone be, Shamar." I started to play stupid again, but one look at his face had me swallowing and closing my eyes before I started talking.

"I have an aunt… my daddy's baby sister. Tavion and I love her to death, but she won't really associate with us anymore." I began.

"Why?"

"My uncle, well, her husband, is a ho. No other word for it. He done slept around their whole marriage, from what I understand. When she catches him, he either blames her and she accepts it because she's insecure or he lies so much that she doubts herself. She stops believing her own eyes and ears and instincts. But she's embarrassed to be around family because she knows, and she knows we know. So she just stays away and stays with him."

He grilled me. "What that gotta do with us, Shamar?"

4

"Tremell! I *saw* you with my own eyes. I saw that bitch with my own eyes. You keep saying let you explain." I shook my head. "I can't do that. I'm not gon let you make me distrust my own senses. What reasonable explanation can there be for her sucking your dick in public? And even if she did somehow 'set you up,' what made you ready to fall for it? You not a naïve man. You *knew* she wanted you. Everyone knows that, hell." I crossed my arms over my chest. "So, I'm not gon fall into the trap that my TeTe Amber does. I gotta keep that much self-respect."

His head was resting on the back of the couch as he listened. He stroked his beard and thought about what I had said. Finally, he spoke, without even looking at me. "Yo, that shit he does, ma? That's called gas lighting. I wouldn't never do no foul shit like that to you. I fucked up, true. But, I ain't fucked another chick, ain't barely looked at one since I been rocking with you. I don't lie to you and I've done everything I promised to you. So for you to compare me to a fuckboy like your uncle?" He shook his head.

I watched quietly as he stood up. I wanted to grab on to him so badly… but I just couldn't.

He looked down at me for a minute and I could see hurt and anger battling in his eyes. "You said you trusted me. You lied-"

"I have to trust myself, Tremell," I said softly.

"Do that, shorty. I won't try to explain again," he said.

I missed him before the door even closed behind him.

(One Year Earlier)

I never expected to find myself in this position at 19, but I can't lie, I was excited. Last year, I met the man of my dreams when we were both French tutors at a local university. It turned out that he and his twin were like me and were really good with languages. He spoke five, while I spoke eight. We started off talking about that and pretty soon, we were inseparable. So here I was, a year later, dancing around my apartment and laughing to myself. I couldn't wait until Tamir got here so I could surprise him. I flopped down on the couch to text him.

ME:

Baby!

MON COEUR (YEP, I HAD HIM SAVED AS THE FRENCH WORDS FOR "MY HEART." MY DADDY WAS FROM MARTINIQUE, AFTER ALL):

What it do, shawty?

ME:

You are so corny!

MON COEUR:

But you love my corny ass. What's up, ma?

ME:

You were supposed to be here by now. Hurry up!

MON COEUR:

Damn, Bae! I'ma put it down when I get there. Don't worry.

ME:

eyeroll emoji Nigga, I got a surprise for you.

MON COEUR:

Oh, yeah? I'll be there in a little bit, I promise. I'm working on a surprise for you, too.

ME:

Really? Just hurry!

MON COEUR:

Bye, girl. I luh you, my beautiful, brown baby.

ME:

purple heart emojis

I lay back on the couch and closed my eyes to wait on him. The next thing I knew, I was being awakened by his kisses. I smiled, threw my arms around his neck, and kissed him back. I loved this boy with everything in me. I couldn't believe I'd been lucky enough to find him this early in life. And now…

"Mir, what's my surprise?" I asked as he gave me one last kiss and walked across the room to put his keys in the bowl.

"Swear you the most impatient thang in the world, DuBois. Chill!" He sounded like he was scolding me, but he was smiling. I took a minute to revel in how beautiful he was. Like all his siblings, he was gorgeous, golden-caramel toned, and tall as hell. Mir sported locks and claimed his hair made people weak. He had light brown eyes and the cutest dimples. But his smile… that was everything. He had lips I loved to kiss and the prettiest, straightest white teeth. He reminded me of Boris Kodjoe, not that I was biased. My boo was fine too. He had the body of a runner, all long, lean muscles. I watched as he stripped off his shirt. I licked my lips.

"Calm down, you little freak," he said, then started laughing. "Look."

I looked. On the left side of his chest, just above his heart, he had a new tattoo. It was a picture of me. Below the image were the words, "*Ma Martiniquaise.*" I burst out crying and ran to him, pressing kisses all over his chest. "I love you. It's so beautiful!"

"Of course it is, shorty. It's an image of you. Now where my surprise?"

Oh! I had almost forgotten. I jumped back and clapped my hands. "Guess!"

He gave me a goofy smile. "Shiiiiiit. Where that vintage Maybach at, ma?"

I rolled my eyes. "You must gone loan me the money to buy it for you?" Both of us started laughing then and he grabbed me into a hug. "I'm out of guesses, DuBois. Just tell me," he said, kissing my forehead.

"Ok," I said, unable to hide my big ass grin. But before I could tell him, someone was banging on the door. Mir reached for the gun he kept in his back. He put his finger against his lips, signaling for me to be quiet. I nodded and watched as he crossed the room quietly and flung open the door, gun cocked and ready. I saw a girl I didn't know, but apparently he did, because he said,

8

"What the fuck you doing here?" I'd never heard him talk to a woman like that before.

"Chill, Mir. You ain't gotta shoot me. I just came to meet step mama."

He frowned down at her. "What the hell you talking about with your dizzy ass, Daria?" "I'm pregnant, Tamir. And it's yours."

Suddenly, everything inside me fell apart. I felt light-headed, like all the blood left my body. Tamir's voice sounded distant as he said, "You a damned lie, you silly ass ho. Don't ever come to my shorty's crib disrespecting us like that! I oughta bust on your ass for real, Daria!"

Please, God. The one thing I'd asked Mir never to do was cheat on me. If he didn't want me, he could be honest. And then I snapped to my senses. They were standing in *my* apartment arguing like I wasn't even there. They were so damned loud that Tamir didn't even hear me calling him at first. Finally, after my third attempt, he turned and walked to me. "Baby, this bitch is lying."

"So it's not yours?" I asked.

"Hell, nah, shorty!" He said with much attitude. "She probably ain't even pregnant."

I smiled in relief… until I thought about the alternative question. "Mir, *could* it be yours?"

He didn't answer that one. My knees buckled and he caught me. "DuBois, listen." I couldn't listen. All I could see was that bitch standing in my house smirking. I pulled out of his arms and grabbed her. I didn't give a fuck about her being pregnant or nothing else as I started punching her in her head, her throat, her face, anywhere I could find. She was screaming, begging Tamir to get me off her, calling me a crazy bitch. It took all of Tamir's strength to pull me back and then I started whaling on his ass. These motherfuckers had just destroyed my life. I called Tamir everything but a child of God as I sobbed and punched. He let me wear myself down, until I was so tired that I was just an exhausted, crying mess. That bitch had had sense enough to leave, at least. And now it was his turn. He betrayed me and I was done. "Get out! *Ne me touche pas!*"

"Don't touch you? DuBois, can we at least talk? I'm sorry, baby. So sorry. I never wanted to hurt you."

"There is nothing to explain. Leave me the fuck alone!" I said, struggling until I broke free from his arms. Crossing the room, I grabbed his keys, and threw them at his head. Unfortunately, he caught them.

"Fine. I'ma let your crazy ass calm down. Then we gone talk. I'll be back. I put that on my Mama," he vowed.

"GET THE FUCK AWAY FROM ME!" I screamed. He finally left, but I knew he wasn't lying about coming back. I went to my bedroom and pulled out a suitcase. He paid the rent here; he could decide what to do. I was leaving. As I started packing, I made sure the first thing I threw in the suitcase was my positive pregnancy test.

(*Present Day*)

After all of Tripp and Tre's, my oldest brothers, drama this past weekend. I needed this spa day. I sat back as I waited for my aesthetician to start my facial. I heard the spa owner, Trina, chatting with someone. She called the other customer "Chantal," and my nosy ass had to peek. I was hoping it was my twin brother Tamir's ex. I liked her a lot and I really wanted them to get back together. I sat up to speak to her once I recognized her voice. She was holding a baby, a little girl. She was as beautiful as her mother except... she looked just like me. I felt my smile disappear and I watched as her face fell. "Oh, Chantal," I said. "I know he was wrong. But how could you do this?"

"Tamar," she began, but then she shook her head. Turning, she asked Trina if we could use her office. Trina was genuinely a sweetheart and she ushered us into the room, no questions asked. I turned to Chantal the minute the door was closed. I would never expect no shit like this from her and I was pissed.

"I don't give a damn about you and Tamir's overgrown asses, but she is ours, too, and we have a right to know her. And she has a right to know us."

"I know, Tay. I know. I'm not gone lie. I was pissed at first and didn't want to have to co-parent with him. But, as time passed, I just didn't know how to tell him. And I knew he was gone be furious after she got here. I swear I've been thinking about how to tell him, especially since he got shot. I never meant for him to leave this earth without knowing her."

"The best way to tell him is *just to tell him*, Chan. Yeah, he gone be mad. I'm mad at your ass right now. But there's no use in losing any more time."

She sighed and nodded.

"My first niece and I don't even know her name or how old she is."

"Her name is Noah-"

"His middle name," I said softly. Even now, I felt sorry for her and Mir. They so obviously loved each other, but Chantal's pride and pain stood in the way of their reconciliation. That, and the fact that Mir had gone on a binge since they broke up, fucking anything with a pussy, I swear. I know he was trying to erase her from his mind, though. He was failing miserably.

"She's almost six months old."

"You have her looking so sweet," I complimented. The baby had on a little purple sundress and the most adorable tiny sandals in the world. "She's gorgeous."

Chantal smiled. "Not that you're biased."

"She does look like her TeTe, doesn't she?" I said, feeling smug. "May I hold her?"

"Of course."

Noah fretted for a minute—she didn't know me, after all. But after I cooed to her and rocked her, she settled against me. "You know I have to tell him."

"Yeah… I know."

"It's time, Chan."

The Kinsey men plus Tavion were gathered in my parents' game room. My brother Ty and I shot pool. Pops and Tavion were talking business—little nigga was a math and accounting wiz and he was turning out to be an excellent money launderer using our other businesses. We were proud of the kid. I had to laugh. Only we would be proud of someone becoming a better criminal. Tripp and Tre sat on one of the couches looking pitiful. I felt sorry for them niggas, but they had no sympathy when they bluesed me about DuBois. So I couldn't resist…

"Y'all see these long-faced, heart-aching niggas over here?" I asked, laughing. Tre mugged me.

"Shut up, nigga, before I cut your face in half," he said. He probably would have if I wasn't his brother.

"You ain't lying, Mir. I can't believe I raised these niggas. Sitting in here looking like hound dogs. If you that sick, go get your women. Hell, Tripp, go get your family!" Pops said.

"My family don't want me," Tripp said. This nigga sounded sad!

"You just rolling over like that?" Ty asked. "You just gone let them go?"

"Cyn let me go, hell."

Pops shook his head. "Niggas, are your balls even there anymore?" Tre clenched his jaw, but he knew Pops was the one person in the world who would take one of these cue sticks and beat the hell out of him if he acted froggy. Well, Mama probably would, too.

"Ol' heart broke niggas," I said, still laughing. Tripp started to stand up. "Don't think I won't bust you upside your head with this stick then kick your ass," I told him. My phone rang. I pulled it out of my pocket and looked at the screen. Tamar. I tapped to accept her call. I put her on speaker because I knew she didn't want nothing but to act like I was six-years-old and she was my mama. My twin refused to accept the fact that I was healed.

"What, ol' worrisome girl?"

"Hey, Mir."

"Hey, Tay," I mocked her.

"What you doing?"

"Chilling with fam. Where you at?"

"Just left the spa. Guess who I ran into?" she asked.

"Who?" I asked, racking up the balls.

"Chantal."

I hesitated. Just for a second, but long enough for everyone to notice.

"Who looking sick now, nigga?" Tre said. I ignored him.

"So?" I said, acting like I didn't give a fuck.

"Mir, Chantal has a baby."

Suddenly, I knew what swallowing acid must feel like. It couldn't have hurt more if DuBois had carved my heart out with a rusty spoon. If this is how she felt when Daria pulled that bullshit, I don't blame her for running away. My vision and hearing dimmed as rage spread through me. Her babies were supposed to be *mine*. The thought of her laying up with someone else and carrying that nigga's kids made me sick. But I wasn't gone show these niggas nothing, even though all of them were looking at me like they felt sorry for me.

"She told me she was seeing someone. I guess she was more than seeing, huh?" I said, and laughed. Fake ass me.

"Tamir," she paused. "Her baby looks just like us and her name is Noah."

I stood up slowly from the table. "What the fuck?" I heard Ty say.

"What you saying, Tay?"

Her voice got soft. "You *know* what I'm saying, brother."

I was Tamir. The mellow Kinsey. The joking one. The one with the best attitude. But that didn't stop me from throwing the fucking phone across the room and watching it shatter against the wall. "I know she didn't do that. I know that bitch didn't hide my seed from me," I said. I started walking toward the door. Pops grabbed me.

"You gone have to calm down, son," he said.

"Nah. No calm. No chill, Pops. That shit is foul. I know I fucked up, but she ain't right."

"Where you think you going, nigga?" Tripp asked, coming to stand in front of me

"Where the fuck you think I'm going? To meet my shorty and probably fuck her mama up."

Tripp shook his head. "You can't go like this. You can't let the first time you meet your baby be while you mad. Kids sense that shit. You gone make her scared."

"So now you the baby whisperer because you played daddy a few months?" I probably deserved that punch he landed upside my head. But that didn't stop me from squaring up with that nigga. It took everybody in the room to pull us apart. Fighting Tripp's ass didn't stop my attitude.

"Fuck!" I yelled. "I got a baby. I got a daughter named after me and I don't even know her."

Ty grabbed my shoulder. "But you will. Chill, man. You gone get to know your shorty. We all are."

I knew he was telling the truth. Wasn't no way DuBois was gone continue to keep my seed from me. But that didn't make me feel no better. Suddenly, everyone's phones sounded off. Tre checked his message first. This nigga smiled, something that never happened. He walked over to me and handed me his phone. "Look."

I looked down. Tay had apparently sent a group text with a picture of baby girl. She was beautiful—same color as all of us, chunky and smiling, with big, pretty eyes and a head full of hair. That shit calmed me down. "She do look just like Tay. Of course, a nigga would make a beautiful baby," I said, memorizing every detail about her.

"Them Kinsey genes," Pop said proudly. "You put in work, son."

They all laughed, then, but I kept staring at my little mama. I had a baby. "Yo, I got a daughter, y'all. Fuck all you niggas and ya weak ass sperm. Your baby brother got a little one before any of you!" I bragged.

"Don't make me fuck you up again," Tripp said. "That shit just means yo pull out game weak as hell."

Tre shook his head. "First, Cynaa and now Noah. Them baby girls gone blues y'all."

Yeah, seeing my little one made me happy. But DuBois was still gone feel my wrath. I couldn't even be as mad as I should be, though. I remember when she came to see me in the hospital, and I noticed how her breasts were a little bigger and her hips had spread. Knowing her body had changed to grow and feed my youngin', knowing that she had to bear and birth my seed—that shit was doing something to a nigga head. Like, I hated her for what she did…

But I loved her beautiful ass, too.

"Mir?" Tripp said.

"It's all good, nigga," I cut him off. "I'll wait til tomorrow. I don't wanna upset my baby."

Tripp was shaking his head. "Nah. I was wrong. If we know about Chantal and Noah, Prince might be just a few hours behind us. You need-"

I lurched forward. I didn't even have to hear him complete that sentence. I needed to go get my family.

I was tired. Knowing that Tamir was eventually coming but not knowing when, drained all the little energy I'd had today. I know Tay probably called him the minute we left the spa. I kept checking my rearview mirror, expecting to see someone following me. Would he try to take her? Keep her from me as payback? Truth is, I'd never had Tamir really, really angry at me. What I'd seen of him in the streets was terrifying though. It was like he completely changed. Mir was so laid back, with the best sense of humor, and sweet as could be. But when he got angry over work, I don't know who he became. He was ice-cold, his voice was different, and his smile disappeared. I'd never met their brother, Tre, but I'd heard of him. Ty once told me, "Everybody think Tripp is the one as crazy as Tre. Nah. Your nigga shoulda been Tre's twin instead of Tamar's."

I swallowed as I lifted Noah from her changing table, remembering Ty's comment. Would he treat me like that? Like a random bitch in the streets? I settled in the rocking chair to nurse my baby, my mind going crazy. I knew she could feel my tension because she was whining and fidgeting. My baby was typically happy and smiling, especially when her chubby self was eating. I needed to get out my supplies and paint or sketch, but my nerves probably wouldn't let me concentrate.

"What's going to happen, *bébé*? What will your *papa* do, hmm?" I whispered to her. She babbled a little, relaxing as I talked to her. I was glad she didn't know what I was saying exactly. Her little eyelids worked hard to stay open, but they soon lost the battle. She didn't even wait to be burped. I put her on my shoulder and rocked with her a little bit. Finally, exhausted, I climbed into bed, cradling my baby.

———

"Wake your trifling ass up and pack some shit for you and my shorty. Fast."

I woke up with a jerk and almost screamed as Tamir stared at me from the foot of my bed. He was mugging me, his arms crossed over his chest. I sat up, instinctively pulling Noah into my arms. His eyes went to her immediately and his face softened. He seemed more like himself as he looked at our baby. Suddenly, the seriousness of what I had done slammed into me. I felt guilty as hell. He'd hurt me… hell, I *still* hurt. But we didn't have to interact all that much for him to be in our daughter's life. Both of us were wrong in how we'd treated each other and our daughter was the one who would have to suffer for it.

"Give me my shorty and go do what I said," he ordered, walking to the side of the bed and extending his hands. I carefully placed our sleeping little one in his arms. He smiled as he pulled her to his chest, rocking her gently.

"I know that you might want to spend some time with her, but I'm not going anywhere with you, Tamir," I said softly.

He shrugged. "I really don't give a fuck. My family and I are at war with some dangerous people who look for any sign of weakness and try to hit us there. My baby will not be staying here for somebody to come along and kidnap her to use as leverage. So get her a few things together and I can buy whatever else she needs. You can stay wherever the fuck you want.

Knowing how I got in here and you didn't even wake up, it shouldn't take them long to sneak up on you. After they send about 10 dudes to rape you and beat your ass, they'll make you call me. And I won't answer, bitch. So, it's up to you."

I couldn't even hide the tears that came to my eyes as he shredded my heart again. Oh, God, he'd *never* talked to me like that and he sounded so serious. I climbed out of the bed and moved past him so he couldn't see my hurt. Without a word, I packed a few clothes and pairs of shoes for both of us, some of the frozen breast milk I had expressed, and my pump. I grabbed some of my baby's other items and pushed them into a diaper bag. It didn't even take me ten minutes. With my back to him, I said, "I'm ready. We just gotta get her car seat."

uck! I just wanted to hurt her like she hurt me. If a nigga ever laid hands on her to rape her or hit her, I wouldn't rest until I fed him his balls. But that look on her face before she blanked her expression had almost killed me. I knew she was about to cry. She moved around the house quietly as I loved on my little mama. Noah was perfect, so beautiful that it almost hurt to look at her. She smelled sweet and she snuggled up to me in her sleep. I couldn't help kissing her forehead and her little eyes. After a few minutes, DuBois had a suitcase and a couple of bags at her feet.

"I'm ready," she said, her voice empty. "We just gotta get her car seat."

I wanted to say something to her. I wanted to apologize. I wanted to drop down and kiss her feet for growing the doll in my arms. But I also wanted to punish her, make her understand the hurt that was running through me.

So, I stayed quiet, and handed her the baby. I started picking up her stuff. "You can go ahead outside. My car is out there and I got a man in a Benz watching the house. Let him in your car to get her car seat."

She nodded and said nothing as she walked out. Austin retrieved Noah's car seat and put it in my back seat. DuBois buckled her in and then moved to open the front door. She gave me a little smile. "You got the Maybach, huh?" she said, talking about my Mercedes-Maybach S600. I gave her a quick nod and walked off, acting like I didn't see her face fall. I wanted to change the subject.

Before she realized my car was her favorite shade of emerald green.

I slid into the driver's seat and glanced at her as she stared out the side window.

"Where are we going?" she asked.

I had meant to take them to River Oaks, to my parents'. That's where I mostly crashed and I knew they were all ready to see Noah. But I changed my mind. First of all, it was too damned busy since my parents were having a Fourth of July party tomorrow. Second, I'd copped a place of my own a few months ago. It didn't have much furniture, and none of them pictures and curtains shit she liked, but I wanted to take my family to my own place. *Family?* I almost laughed at myself. She and I could barely speak to each other. Not good for "family."

"You can't even tell me that, Tamir?"

I sighed. "Home, DuBois. We're going home."

TREMELL

I stood on the porch of a small, but neat house. It was surrounded by flowers and bushes and had some kind of full tree in the yard. I knocked on the door. A few seconds later, a sweet voice asked, "Who is it?" No use telling her my name. She wouldn't know me. But I wanted to make sure she opened the door.

"I'm here about Shamar Parker." I heard her run toward the door and then she was yanking it open.

"Oh, my God, is she okay?" the woman asked. I could hear that she was really concerned.

I looked at her for a moment. She was a pretty, heavyset woman, with medium brown skin, Shamar's big, pretty eyes, and natural hair pulled back by a band.

"Are you Amber?"

"Is she okay?" she repeated.

I stood there, showing her that I was as stubborn as she was. She sighed and gave in. "Yes, I'm Amber. Now, tell me-"

"I'm her boyfriend, Tre Kinsey. I came to talk to you because you fuckin' up our relationship."

Her eyes widened and she put a hand on her breasts. "That's kinda rude."

"But the truth. I'ma tell you some shit, then I want you to talk to my girl."

Amber pursed her lips and mugged me. Finally, she stepped back and let me in. "After you," she said, holding out her hand.

I shook my head. "Uh-uh, Shorty. I'on give nobody my back." She rolled her eyes, but she moved ahead of me. She led me into a nicely decorated living room. It wasn't fancy, but it looked homey, like some sentimental shit Mouse would like. I had barely sat down before she was questioning me.

"How is my niece? And how am I ruining your relationship?"

I leaned forward and put my elbows on my thighs. "See, I'm wondering why you don't know how your niece, who loves you very much, is doing?"

She looked embarrassed as she shrugged. "We've both just been busy. I love her very much, too. Her and Tavi. They're all I have left-"

"You need to act like it!"

Amber mugged me. "I don't understand how my relationship with my niece has anything to do with your relationship."

I smirked, then broke down what Mouse had explained to me. By the time I finished she was crying. *Shit! This where that girl gets all that damned bawling from.*

"Look, I ain't come to upset you. I just want you to reach out to my girl. You don't seem miserable to me. Maybe your husband fucks around cause you do, too." She gasped and opened her mouth to say something, but I didn't wait. "Or maybe you don't wanna be bothered. Or maybe that nigga is fucking over you and you're a damned doormat."

"Mr. Kinsey!!!" she looked like she wanted to faint.

"Whatever it is, if you care about your niece and happiness, you need to call her or visit her and let her know you a happy, willing doormat." She just shook her head.

I stood up. "And do it soon," I ordered.

First, she looked at me like she wanted to object. But after I grilled her, she said, "Okay," in a soft voice.

"Glad we understand each other, seeing as how we gone be family." I decide to throw her a bone. I ain't all hard ass. "Shamar and Tavi ain't all you got left. Your niece is pregnant. She needs you."

I left her there with a smile on her face.

(Three weeks later)

My now two-times-a-week lunches with Aaron almost pushed me to tears. Bless his heart, he loved our daughter and I knew he cared about me. But there was only so much I could listen to about his life and his plans and his uncle Alonzo Prince. I refused to think about why he gushed about Prince now and I hadn't even known their connection a month ago.

We sat in Brennan's and I was preoccupied pushing my shrimp and grits into different patterns on my plate. I kept glancing at my phone. Even now, even though I knew it was wrong, I always hoped to look down and see Tristan calling or texting me. I missed him, despite knowing that I couldn't have him.

"You don't like it?" Aaron asked.

I snapped out of my thoughts. "Huh?"

"The shrimp and grits. You don't like the food? Because I can get you something else." He already had his hand halfway up in the air before I shook my head.

"I'm fine. Just not hungry, really," I said.

He looked at me like he knew I was lying. But instead of calling me on that shit, he just shook his head and took a bite of his crab cake. I jumped as he let his fork clatter against his plate. "Look, Cyn. I know you think you had feelings for that- that

26

thug. But if I hadn't been awake, he would've killed our baby. You need to put him out your mind-" he reached over to grab my hand. "And think about what I suggested."

What he suggested... A reconciliation. Aaron said we should make a family where our little girl would have both her parents.

Except, our little girl and I cried for Tripp every day. I didn't know how to comb her baby doll's hair right. Only Tripp. I didn't know how to sing with her. Only Tripp. I knew she wasn't trying to hurt my feelings, but damn. And, truth be told, I missed him every night. Wanted his kisses and his touches and his sense of humor. Missed seeing him chomp down extra hard on that toothpick when I pissed him off. Missed cuddling next to him while he complained but watched every chick flick I chose. Missed him being on top of me, inside me, spooning me.

"There you go again!" Aaron said, squeezing my hand a little too hard. I yanked away from him and was ready to knock the hell out of him when my phone chimed. Given my social media status, I was used to plenty of alerts, but this was a text chime. I snatched my phone up, trying not to get my hopes up.

It was Devyn. I bit back a sigh of disappointment. I loved my bestie, plus he was keeping Cynaa right now. I had no business wishing this text was from someone else. I opened my messages.

DEV:

Bitch!

I started typing.

ME:

What?

27

DEV:

> She sick and she crying for you and her
> daddy.

ME:

> On our way! We're here together.

DEV:

> Did I say her father? I meant her
> DADDY—Tripp.

Swear I hated him.

I looked over at Aaron. "That's Devyn. He said Cynaa ain't feeling well. I should go-" I started to stand up and he placed a hand over mine.

"Is she sick, Cyn, or does he just not want you with me?"

I glared at him. "Does it matter right now? I mean, shouldn't we just check in on her?" I asked. "I told you her ears are bothering her." He at least had the decency to look ashamed.

"You're right. I have some business to handle, but text me how she's doing and I'll swing by later," he said. Text him? Business was more important than his seed? I gave him a cold ass nod before damn near running out the door and to my car. I noticed a heavily tinted SUV following me. These days, I didn't know if it was Aaron or Tripp trying to protect me and I really didn't care. As long as my baby was safe…

She was crying when I made it and, for all his clucking and cooing to her, I knew Devyn was glad to hand her to me. Cynaa was a little warm and she kept rubbing at her ear. Her pediatrician had given her a prescription for an ear infection yesterday, but apparently, it was slow acting. I walked back and forth with her and hummed. She was fretful, but it helped a little bit. God, I knew I was in for a long night.

Tristan

I looked down at my phone where it sat in the treadmill's cupholder as the message notification appeared. I frowned at the unknown number, but checked the text anyway, as I kept walking.

> **832-555-7437:**
>
> You need to go see about your family. Meaning Cyn and Naa.

My heart dropped for a minute as I thought about Prince having them and trying to hold them over my head.

Then, I remembered. Cynaa, my love bug, *was* a Prince. I sped up for a minute. Then, I decided to text back.

> **ME:**
>
> Who the fuck is this?

> **832-555-7437:**
>
> Devyn. Naa is sick and Cyn is out of it.

> **ME:**
>
> She reconciling with her baby daddy. Call that nigga.

> **832-555-7437:**
>
> SMH. You gotta step up your surveillance.

I didn't bother responding to that. Instead, I increased the speed again.

832-555-7437:

> Well, if you decide to get out ya feelings
> and check on them, they at the house.
> But I'm sure you know that.

I ignored that shit, too. I wasn't entertaining whatever the hell Devyn was talking about. Cyn told me to stay away from them. At first, I had no intention of listening to her. I loved her stubborn ass and I knew she loved me. I could wait her out; I didn't care how long it took. And I'd prove to her that I would protect her and Cynaa with my own life.

But then she threw a curveball at me. The last time I texted her, she finally responded. I'd never forget her words. She'd tried to sound all hard and formal: *Tristan, you have to stop contacting me. Aaron and I are going to see if we can put our daughter's well-being first and work on making up.* I think I was drunk for a week straight after that. My brothers came by to make sure I was alive. My Pops came by to talk shit to me. Tamar came by and I swear if she ever tells anyone how I almost broke down... But at the end of the week it was my moms who kicked my ass into gear. She told me I had two options: Go get her or get over her. When I saw Cyn having lunch with her weak ass baby daddy the next day, I made my choice.

But now, here come Devyn's ass with this. Even as I fought it, I knew I needed to see my little bit. I'd take every illness in the world rather than have her be sick. I had no idea of what he meant by, "Cyn is out of it," and I wasn't going to push to find out. Yeah, I told myself as I jumped off the treadmill and took a quick shower, this was all about the baby. I repeated that lie all the way to her house—I was glad the evening rush hour had passed because I was impatient. I parked and got out. Halfway to her door, I heard someone say, "Say nigga, you can't go in-" A soft popping noise let me know those were that nigga's last words. I knew my team would probably have the body gone before I stepped foot in the house. What kind of weak ass detail did Aaron have set up?

I barely knocked once before Devyn yanked the door opened. Ignoring his smirking ass, I immediately made eye contact with Cyn where she stood across the room, holding a whining Cynaa. "What's wrong with her?" I asked, walking toward them. Once she heard my voice, my ladybug turned in her mama's arms and reached for me. "Tripp," she said and started crying. Her little face was puffy and reddened and I had to try to fight back anger. I grabbed her out of Cyn's arms and just rocked her. "It's ok. I'm here. I got you." I sang one of our little silly songs to her. When I felt her start to calm down, I turned back to Cyn. She looked tired and skinny and like she was about to cry herself. Everyone dressed down sometimes, especially at home. But Cyn Murray in a t-shirt that swallowed her and leggings with holes? That wasn't my concern, though. "Yo, why her face look like that, shorty?"

She opened her mouth to reply, but Devyn reappeared with a cool towel that he gave to me. "Because she been crying all day for you. All day, every day, hell," he muttered.

"Devyn!" Cyn said, mugging him. I felt my face twist up, but I focused on soothing the baby's face with the rag.

"For real, Cyn Claire? That's how you coming? You gone let her make herself sick to prove a point?" I didn't even look at her as I asked the questions.

"Well, I guess my work here is done!" Devyn said cheerfully. He gave Cyn a quick hug, then looked at me. "Can I hug you? Maybe pat you on that fine ass?" he asked.

"Nigga, if you don't get yo stupid ass on!" Devyn shrugged, totally unmoved by my mug.

31

"Straight men and their fragile masculinity," he said before leaving the house.

Cyn finally found her voice again. "You know you have to leave, Tristan." She didn't even sound convinced herself. I shook my head. "Nah, shorty. My little bit is sick, been crying for me, and you look like hell, Cyn City. I ain't going nowhere. Go get in the bed before your ass fall over." I could tell she wanted to argue, but then her shoulders dropped. Cyn, giving in and refusing to argue? That shit worried a nigga. I followed her into the bedroom. I watched as she pulled back the covers and slid towards the middle. *Good. She knows the routine, even when she pretends like she don't miss it.* Very gently, I lay Cynaa next to her. She immediately started whimpering and reaching for me. "Shh," I told her. "I'm not leaving you." I planned to sit in the chair against the wall until they fell asleep. But Cynaa wasn't having it. She started crying for real and I scooped her back up before sitting down in the chair. I rocked her and talked to her until she fell asleep. Cyn watched us the whole time.

Finally, when the baby's breaths were long and even, she said something. "Tristan, you know this is wrong. Aaron-"

"Is only alive because of my love bug. Don't bring that nigga up to me," I snapped. I felt her tense up.

"You don't tell me-"

"Go to sleep!"

Cyn did something I don't think I've ever seen her do before. She obeyed.

I thought back to what my pops had said a few weeks ago. *"Go get your family."*

Yeah. Cyn and Cynaa were *my* family, not Aaron's.

And she was gon start acting like it.

TYRESE

Even though Tamir was sometimes closest in attitude to Tre, my mama always claimed my little brother and I were "thick as thieves." She was right. And I knew something was up with Mir, something to do with him getting shot. He wasn't telling me everything, but I was going to find out. So here I was, on a Wednesday evening, pulling my G-Wagen into a spot in a garage attached to one of the Texas Medical Center buildings. Within a few minutes, I was outside the office of Mir's surgeon, Dr. Elyse Rose. I smiled as I got ready to use the key that a few, well-placed bills had gotten me. She was out today, according to my source. I almost regretted that, but I knew I could probably find out more from looking at her files that questioning her. I wouldn't mind seeing her pretty face, though. I'd seen her a few times when Mir was still in the hospital and she reminded me of a well-rounded Lauren London. She acted like she couldn't get away from me fast enough. At the same time, I caught her staring at a nigga more than once. Like most women, the little doctor was feeling me. I debated making her admit it, but I'd leave the bougie, smart chicks to Tre. I liked women who liked to get down.

I looked around before easing my way into her space. It was neat—no surprise—and carried her sweet scent. Her desk was clear, shelves neatly filled with books and vases and other decorative stuff. She had a few pictures—looked like her with her parents and siblings. I was low-key checking to see if she had some with a nigga, but I didn't see any. *Get ya mind right*, I told myself. I turned my focus to the computer on her desk. Sliding into her chair, I worked quickly to gain entry. I'd been hacking into computers for half my life and hers presented no real difficulty. Luckily, she had a Mac which meant I could Air Drop the info to my phone. I started the transfer and got up to walk to a little back corner of her office where her degrees were framed and displayed. She had a Bachelor of Science in Biology, Honors from UT-Austin. Her medical degree was from Baylor. Shorty was smart as hell. I turned to look at some of the awards and plaques she had hanging. I noticed that all the diplomas, the awards, and even the name plate on her desk had the name "B. Elyse Rose." What was her first name and why didn't she use it? I only wondered that for a second, though, because all of my interest was suddenly on the door as it opened. I pulled my gun from my back.

Briar

That was strange. I *never* left my door unlocked. My patients' confidentiality was serious to me. I hated getting people in trouble, but I was going to have to ask management to have a talk with maintenance and facilities. Sighing, I closed the door behind me. I was supposed to be off today, but I was bothered by this one case in which a colleague and I were struggling to figure out what was causing a young man's paralysis. I had just noticed my computer was on when a figure stepped out from the back of my office with a gun aimed at me.

I was too shocked to even scream.

"What your little ass doing here?" Tyrese Kinsey asked me with a scowl, lowering his gun.

Finally, I found my voice. "You have a lot of nerve, in my office and questioning my presence. I'm calling security!" This man had broken into my office, but all I could think of was how damned good he looked. He was dressed all in black, from his Polo T-shirt to his Buscemi sneakers. Even the large diamonds in his ears were black. His smooth, caramel skin was gorgeous and he looked so much like a lighter-skinned Future with that smirk on his face and his long, blonde and black locks. They were pulled on top of his head, but the style didn't detract from his masculinity. And, God, that body! He was a work of art. I'd never seen him unclothed, but I could tell he was a dedicated gym-goer. He was thick and solid, his arms massive, his eight-pack outlined beneath the t-shirt. His smile widened. He knew that I was checking him out. I rolled my eyes and reached for my cell phone. "You're going to jail."

"Am I?"

"Yes!" I said, still not dialing.

"Call 'em, Dr. Rose," he taunted.

"I am!" I almost yelled. Shit, I couldn't even remember the number for security, looking at his fine ass. "This is serious. You violated my patients-"

He walked closer to me. "I only needed my brother's file."

"You violated me!" My voice wavered as he came to stand right in front of me. Slowly, he lifted his hand and traced my lips with his thumb. "When I violate you, doctor, you'll know. Because you gon love it," he promised. I lost the ability to breathe as I almost came. I flicked out my tongue, wanting to wet my suddenly dry lips. Instead, my tongue rubbed against his thumb. Salty. Warm. Delicious. He smiled again. "No rush," he whispered. "You'll have plenty of opportunities to taste me."

My breath came back. "I would never-"

"Stop lying. You will. You gone beg me to let you," he said, his tone confident and seductive.

I had to change the subject before I melted. I tried to break the tension by walking to the door and placing a hand on the knob. "Tamir's information is confidential. He'll tell you what he wants you to know. Now, you need to leave." But he was there as I twisted the knob, pressing into the back of me, pulling my hand off the door.

"What's your first name?" he bent down to ask me that in my ear. In a minute, my pussy was going to have soaked straight through my jeans.

"Do you understand the notion of personal space?" I asked,

fighting not to lean back against him. Fuck! He smelled so good! Like forest and cinnamon and sex and… Wait; I wasn't making a damned bit of sense.

"The personal space I'm most interested in right now is here," he said. And he reached around and slid his hand down to cup my sex.

He was absolutely scandalous, unapologetic, and I doubted my legs would hold me up much longer. I wondered if he could feel my pussy throbbing against his hand as he stroked me through my clothes. I was so caught up in my thoughts that it took me a minute to realize that I hadn't told him to move his hand. *I didn't want him to*. "Tyrese… stop," I pleaded.

"I love how my name sounds coming from you. But you won't be telling me stop next time you begging me," he murmured against my ear, just before nipping my ear lobe. I had to lean forward and rest my forehead on the door. This was so crazy. But it felt soooo good.

And then a thought occurred to me. "How old are you?" God! I finished high school early, then it took me two years to get my Bachelors' followed by four years of medical school and a five-year residency. I wasn't old at 27, but I knew he wasn't much older than Tamir who was 21.

"Yeah, I'm younger than you. But that ain't gone stop you from calling me Daddy."

Did I really whimper?

"Tell me your first name," he demanded again.

"B-B-Briar," I stammered.

He surprised me by turning me around. He was grinning. "Seriously?"

I nodded.

"Your name is Briar Rose? Like the fairytale?"

37

I nodded again.

"What kind of corny ass black people you come from?" He asked, laughing out loud. "For real, though, ma? Briar Rose?"

He was doubled over laughing. I narrowed my eyes and crossed my arms over my chest. "Shut up!" I grumbled. "Get out of my office, Tyrese."

He straightened up, still smiling at me. "A'ight, shorty. But I'll be back."

Before I could blink, he'd pressed me against the door and kissed me briefly. My lips tingled as he gently moved me and slipped out the door.

I slid to the floor.

Shamar

I sat up on the examination table while Tremell sprawled in a chair in the cold, sterile room. It was decorated in pinks and blues with alphabet hung along the walls and posters of different pregnancy stages on display. This was our second pre-natal visit. I wanted it to go more smoothly than the first I'd had when I was around eight weeks along. *That* had been a disaster. Tremell was so sure I was going to try to hide something from him, that he was present for everything, even the breast and cervical exams. I was mortified, the doctor was surprised, and he was absolutely determined. The most pressing concern I'd had was my fear that my birth control pills may have hurt my baby, but the doctor reassured me. At first, I couldn't even understand how I was pregnant—well I know *how*—because I took my pills religiously. I'd been on them since I was 17 because of my horrible ass periods. But then, I remembered those days at his house in the Hill Country. No pills for those few days. That had thrown everything off. We were going to have a late January/early February baby. I was scared and excited and elated.

I just wished my baby daddy wasn't a fucking cheat. We sat in complete silence. For the last few weeks we talked as little as possible. He was staying at his parents' until they resolved the situation with Alonzo Prince. That's where he told me he was staying, anyway, since he'd left my house. He probably was laying up with that bitch Katerah. That shit hurt me *and* pissed me off. They deserved each other.

39

But… I had to admit as I looked at his fine ass draped across the chair that the pregnancy increased my sex drive. I wanted to swallow my pride and have him move back to my house so I could fuck him every night. There was only so much a little bullet and my imagination could do. I craved his dick inside me more than any food or whatever else pregnant women were supposed to crave. My eyes traveled to his crotch. Even when it wasn't erect, his dick left an impressive print.

When I looked back up, he was staring at me, smirking. My face turned hot. He palmed himself and he was suddenly semi-erect. Swear my damn mouth watered.

"You miss this dick, shorty? You be a good girl and I'll let you have it. They say pregnant pussy is the best, so I'm ready whenever you are."

I scoffed. "I wouldn't fuck you with somebody else's pussy, after you been laying up with that skank. You not finna give me and my baby no disease!" I rolled my eyes.

He mugged me. "Hey, ma. I'ma fuck you up behind that slick ass mouth. I wouldn't never put you or my seed at risk. And that's *my* pussy. I'ma remind you soon."

Before I could say anything else, there was a knock on the door and Dr. Christine Mason entered. She smiled and greeted us as she washed her hands. It didn't take her long to review the nurse's notes, ask me some questions, and answer a few of ours. Then she clapped her hands.

"Well, mama and daddy, you're right at 12 weeks. I had you change into a gown, Shamar, in case you wanted to hear the baby's heartbeat. Would you like that?" she asked.

I nodded, breathless. Tremell smiled and came to stand beside the table. We watched as she readied the little handheld ultrasound, coating it with gel. She had me lie back, cover my bottom half with a sheet, and pull the gown up above my rounding belly. When I was ready, she started moving the probe across my stomach. Silence. Then suddenly, just as I was about to worry, I heard the most beautiful sound in the world, the fast-paced, rhythmic beat of my baby's little heart. I got tears in my eyes as I looked up at Tremell.

"Ay, yo, Doc? Is it supposed to be fast like that?" he asked.

"Mm-hmm," she said, checking the display. "155 beats per minute. That's normal."

I watched as he smiled. "That shit is dope. That's really my little nigga?"

"Tremell!" I hissed.

"My bad. Our baby. That's really our baby?" Dr. Mason was laughing as she nodded. "Heartbeat of a lion," Tremell bragged. I rolled my eyes even as a couple of happy tears slid down my cheeks.

"You always with that crying, shorty!"

I ignored him and took the paper towels Dr. Mason gave me to wipe my stomach. She told me I could get dressed and she'd be back to wrap up the visit. The moment she was gone, Tremell turned his fitted cap around backwards and bent over to kiss my belly.

"Ay! We made something beautiful, Mouse." More tears came to my eyes as I nodded. He hadn't called me that in weeks. He shook his head at me, then reached in the pocket of his jeans and withdrew a small box that he threw into my lap.

"What's this?" I asked.

He rolled his eyes. "Open it."

I did. And my jaw dropped. Attached to an 18-karat, white gold chain was a Circle of Life pendant, adorned with yellow diamonds. It was beautiful. And the meaning of the yellow diamonds…

He shrugged and cleared his throat. "So I been looking up what's some good shit that a baby daddy should buy while his girl is pregnant and that Circle of Life shit kept coming up because you giving my seed life and a circle represents eternity and so there you go and I swear to God you better not do all that damned crying."

I stared at him as tears rolled down my cheeks. I'd never get used to how nervous he got when he tried to express his feelings. "That was the most awkward shit I ever heard in my life and it was beautiful. Just like this necklace. Put it on me."

"Shit! You won't let me," he muttered.

"Tremell! Put *the necklace* on me." He did as I asked. He was always so gentle now, like he was scared I was gone break.

"Thank you," I told him softly. "I love it."

"Enough Oprah shit. Put your damned clothes on."

I rolled my eyes at him. "I'm still mad at you."

He tilted his head and looked at me. Then he gave me that cocky ass smile. "You gone get over it."

"I don't know, Tremell."

He gave me a serious look then. "You might as well. Ain't neither one of us going nowhere, Mouse. I'm not letting you leave me behind some shit you never would let me explain."

I shook my head.

"Now hurry up with them damned clothes. Me and my little one ready to eat."

T hree weeks of barely talking. Of avoiding each other. Of living together but only existing. He had said we were going home. But this house, as lovely as it was, was not a home, even though he'd given me obscene amounts of money and a Reserve card to decorate it as I pleased. It was too quiet and too cold. The only thing that brought me peace was seeing Tamir build a relationship with our daughter. She recognized her *papa* now, smiled at him and cooed for his attention. And he doted on her. In fact, he seemed in awe of her.

We'd tried, a week ago, to go out together. Just to his favorite store—Target. I was pushing around a cart with our baby in her carrier when the first of his tricks smirked at us while she walked with a friend.

"Heeeey, Tamir," she said.

He gave me a nervous look before throwing up his chin at them. "Wazzam, Teryah?"

She put a hand on her hip. "I haven't heard from you lately. I guess you been playing daddy?" She and her friend giggled like they were being smart.

My temper rose all the way up. "Bitch, he ain't playing. This is his daughter, you-"

Tamir grabbed my arm, then addressed his ho. "Chill, Ryah. This my baby mama and my little one. Don't come at them like that."

She looked me and my baby up and down and I moved to

choke the bitch. Mir grabbed me again. He looked at me and shook his head.

She smirked again. "Y'all cute. But if you ever get tired of being tied down, hit me up, Mir. You know how we get down." She blew him a kiss before switching her ass off. He wouldn't let me go to go after she walked off.

"Yo, DuBois, why you trippin'? I'm clearly with you and my little shorty."

Tears sprang to my eyes. "You let her disrespect us," I said, yanking away from him. Swear I threw thousands of dollars' worth of unnecessary shit in my basket and made him pay for it while I refused to speak to him.

I think we both silently agreed we should never go out together again. Tay's voice snapped me back to the present.

"You look so sad, Chan. I hate seeing you like that. You and Mir have to stop this shit," Tamar said. She stood in front of a window, bouncing Noah in her arms.

From my spot curled up on the gray leather sofa, I just smiled at her and turned my attention back to my sketch pad. "We don't like or trust each other. It's not going to get any better."

Tamar rolled her eyes. "Lies and more lies. You and Mir ain't fooling nobody but each other." I just shook my head. I didn't want to talk about Tamir. Talking about him hurt. Being close to him hurt. Seeing the way he looked at me hurt. Loving him hurt.

"Listen, do me a favor," Tay said. I looked at her expectantly. "Weren't you seeing somebody recently?" She walked over and sat beside me.

Before Tamir had stormed back into our lives, I'd been dating a nice guy named Aiden. We'd never messed around beyond a few kisses, but I liked spending time with him. I didn't have the same initial spark with him that I'd had with Tamir, but look how that turned out. At 28, he was a little older than I was, but I liked the calm and maturity.

"Yeah," I said.

"Why don't you go out with him again? See if you feel the same way you did when Tamir wasn't in the picture. If you do, fine. You can pursue that. But if you don't… you need to figure out what that means."

I don't know how Tamar came up with it, but it kinda made sense. Or maybe I just wanted to get out.

Still, I said, "Is that fair to Aiden, the guy I was dating, though?"

"Yes. Because what if he's over there in limbo? Doesn't he deserve to know if you're done with him?"

I thought about what she said for a minute before nodding my agreement.

"Good. The best TeTe in the world is here, right, Noah? Give Te-Tay suga!" She kissed my baby's nose and we both smiled as Noah laughed. "I can babysit. So, go call him now."

My eyes widened. "Now? But I-"

"What? Need to mope around this house while Tamir out doing whatever he does?"

Ooh… she knew how to get me. I'll be damned if I sit up in this house with no life beyond my baby and decorating for him. "You right. Okay," I said.

"Now, don't go crazy. You know dude can't come here. Mir's liable to shoot him. But my detail can shadow you while I stay here with yours." Again, I nodded and reached for my phone. I was going text him.

ME:

Hey. It took a few minutes, but finally, he texted back.

AIDEN:

Hey, Beautiful. Good to hear from you. What's up?

ME:

Would you like to meet me for an early dinner today?

AIDEN:

Just name the place, Lovely.

I smiled. It felt good to be wanted.

S orry, I just had to give Tamir and Chantal a nudge. I knew two things were about to happen:

Chantal was going to realize her new boyfriend was only a diversion from her love for Tamir.

Tamir was finna blow. I smiled at that last thought. He deserved it, hell. Chan was wrong, but if he'd kept his dick in his pants, she wouldn't have run away. And now, he had his daughter and his love (even if he wouldn't acknowledge it) under his roof. He oughta be grateful. Both of them needed to let go of past hurts. What kind of twin sister and friend would I be if I didn't help them?

Noah and I sat, cuddling against the luxurious leather of the couch that Chantal had chosen. I looked around the room done in grays, yellows, and cream. Her taste was impeccable, down to the fresh flowers she placed around the house every day. She was only 20, but she had an eye. I made a note to talk to her about some kind of art or design program. Her interior design skills plus her beautiful paintings and drawings made me believe she could be an incredibly successful artist.

I looked up as Tamir let himself in. My twin was fly as usual, dressed down in an Armani t-shirt and some slim fit Armani jeans. His locks hung in two braids down his back,

"Hey," he said, heading straight for Noah. He swung her up in his arms and nuzzled her cheek.

"Hey, back," I said, pretending to be caught up in changing channels.

"DuBois upstairs?" he asked, as he continued to love on Noah.

"Nope." I made sure my voice was nonchalant. He froze. I waited as he tried to play it off.

"Where she at?" he asked after a minute. "I saw her detail outside-"

"You concerned? Could've sworn she said you told her you wouldn't care if she ended up gang-raped and beaten."

I looked up to meet his eyes finally. They were narrowed and I swear I could almost see smoke coming from his ears. I smiled. "She has my detail. She's fine."

"Where she at, Tay?"

"Where you been, Mir?" I shot back.

"None of your damned business."

"Out doing what the fuck you want and fucking who you want while she spends most of her time here?" I stood up and put my hands on my hips.

"I ain't fucking nobody. And she can go but she gotta keep the detail. She got a baby, anyway. She need to be taking care of our daughter."

I wanted to haul off and slap his ass into the 21st century. "You have a baby, too. Are you trying to do half the work?"

"Tamar. Where. Is. DuBois?" he repeated, pausing after each word.

"Out," I said, then tossed my hair.

He looked like he wanted to hit me, but I knew he wouldn't. Instead, he grilled me and said, "See? That's why I don't half fuck with your smart-mouth ass now."

I rolled my eyes. "Lies you tell. You don't know what you'd do without me."

We stood there, caught in a stand-off as I refused to share my friend's location and he tried to act like he wasn't dying to know where she was. Finally, Mir sighed and rubbed a hand across his locks.

"Can you just tell me out where?"

I shrugged. "Wherever Aiden wanted to take her, I guess."

His jaw dropped.

Checkmate.

Tamir

Who the fuck was Aiden? I wouldn't give Tamar the satisfaction of asking, though, cuz she stood there smirking at me with her arms folded over her chest. My baby mama thought she was about to be all over Houston with some nigga? Nah. She betta hope I didn't catch her laid up with that nigga. I'd dead his ass right in front of her. I might do that anyway. I felt like murdering a nigga. Tamar kept looking at me like it was a fucking joke while I could feel rage boiling through me, ready to erupt on my next unfortunate victim. I was DuBois's first, and as far as I knew, only lover. She had birthed my seed. She lived in my house and I took care of her. She was *mine* and I'll be goddamned if she and my plotting ass sister was gone fuck that up.

I handed Noah back to my twin. She gave me a confused look. "I was about to leave now that you're here."

"I'm sure you volunteered to baby sit, so keep going," I told her. I walked across the room and started jogging up the stairs. I needed to change clothes and get my mind right.

"Tamir? Where are you going? Don't do no stupid shit!" Tay said.

I turned around to look at her. "Y'all shoulda thought about that, huh?"

"What the hell are you tripping about? Y'all not together. Stay claiming you can't stand each other. Won't even talk to each other. Since y'all broke up, you been so free with it, I'm surprised we ain't caught you fucking a wet hole in the ground! But you mad because somebody wanted to take her out and treat her like somebody? And I'll bet your trifling ass think she supposed to go without sex, too. Selfish ass!" Tamar's voice was low because she was holding my daughter, but I knew she wanted to yell. "Fuck you, Mir. I hope that nigga breaks her back!"

I didn't hit women. Even when they hit me, I found a way to restrain their asses. But Tamar's last sentence made something click in my mind. I walked back down the stairs, ready to bust her across her damned face. I stopped a foot away from her. The facts that she had my daughter in her arms and that she was my sister saved her ass from these hands. But it didn't save her from my mouth. "You a stupid, meddling bitch, Tay."

Her eyes flashed, turned black like Tre's did when he was about to body a nigga. She stood there for a moment and I knew she wanted to fight me. It was my turn to smirk at her. "Get my niece," she said, finally. I wanted to refuse, wanted her to stay with Noah while I went to see what the fuck was on DuBois's mind. But Noah was my responsibility. I opened my arms for her and Tay handed her to me.

"I'ma take my bitch ass on," she said.

I was mad at her but when she said that, part of me wanted to apologize. Tay was my twin, my best friend. We argued all the time, but not like this. But damn, she was wishing some other nigga was fucking my... *My what?* And that was the problem. I watched from the doorway as she climbed into her car and Austin rolled out behind her to shadow her. And then I closed the door quietly.

I lasted all of five minutes before I was on the phone. Mama agreed to watch Noah. She had much attitude—not about keeping my baby. She kept saying I was gone do something stupid. She didn't care if I got my stupid self killed but bring her her granddaughter. I just smiled. When I dropped Noah off, Tre hopped in my black Audi S8 Plus. Mama just shook her head and Tamar rolled her eyes at both of us.

TREMELL

I could tell my baby bro was in no mood to talk. That was strange for Mir. But I imagine if Shamar was out with some nigga, even though she claimed we wasn't together, I'd have to rain hell down on Houston. He'd called the team shadowing her and found out that they were at a restaurant called State of Grace, not far from our parents' estate.

"What's the plan, Mir?" I asked, once we'd pulled up and parked. It was his lady, so I was letting him take lead.

"I wanna see what the fuck she doing."

I looked at him for a minute. I knew my expression was saying, "Nigga, what the fuck? Are we brothers?" This little nigga was the one they all swear is just like me, but ain't no way I'd be talking about "seeing what" my shorty was doing out with another nigga. She'd be "seeing" that I wasn't playing no games and that nigga would be getting ready to "see" the roof of somebody's church. Mir stared back at me and shrugged.

"I wanna go in there and blast all that shit. But, she ain't my girl, technically."

"Technically?" This nigga had me fucked up.

He sighed. "Tre, you riding shotgun or nah, man? I don't-"

"I'm just tryna figure out what I'm riding shotgun to," I interrupted him. "I mean, you gone sit back and let this nigga finesse you out ya girl, so what you need me for? Talking about 'technically.' Either she is or she ain't and if she ain't why you got me out here?"

53

"Nigga, you volunteered to come! And I wanna see this nigga. Set some rules. Let him know he better not ever even lay eyes on Noah."

My mouth dropped open in disbelief. I know people think I'm crazy, so maybe my brain was incapable of understanding the shit coming out of my brother's mouth. "You finna meet up with this nigga and set ground rules for how he should date ya girl?" I mean, I can't be the only one who gets a "failure to compute" sign in my head when I hear that.

He slumped down in the seat a little. "She not my girl."

I sighed and reminded myself he was 21. He was still learning.

"Tamir, let me tell you a story."

He started shaking his head fast as hell. "Uh-uh. Fuck, no, Tre. I'm not finna listen to one of ya crazy ass stories!"

That shit shocked me. My stories were perfect. I always made my point. "Who the oldest?" I asked.

"If you tryna bully me into listening, I'ma tell Mama," that punk ass nigga threatened me.

Mama didn't play about her babies, though. I sat back and just stared out the windshield. "Can I just tell you the moral of the story?" I asked after a couple of minutes. He sighed and punched the steering wheel. Man, fuck this lil nigga, missing out on my wisdom. "Quit talking about technicalities and shit. What you wanna do, Mir?"

His face changed. Good. This is the part of me that people saw in him. "What I wanna do? You know what the fuck I wanna do, Tre. I wanna bust up in that bitch, body that stupid ass nigga for even looking at her, then drag her little ass out. I wanna take her home and remind her who Daddy is, make sure she can never forget. That's what the fuck I wanna do." His voice and eyes got colder with every word. I had to stop a proud tear from falling— ok, I'm lying, but yeah, this? *This* was my baby brother.

"So why we sitting here instead of doing that? You got me. That's all you need. I mean, Max watching her on the inside and Darius watching her car, but we ain't even gotta involve them niggas. We can just go get ya girl and I can take care of this nigga who with her later."

He looked at me for a moment. Then, he dapped me up and smiled. "Come on, nigga, with yo scary ass," he said as he jumped out the car. I rolled my eyes and shook my head then followed him. But before we could make it to the front of the restaurant, the door opened. Chantal appeared, looking, as always, like she just stepped off the pages of one of them women's fashion magazines. The nigga behind her, some bougie, stuffed suit looking fucker, was cheesing like he knew he'd hit the jackpot. I heard Tamir make a growling sound. That prompted me to smile—thoughts of murder and mayhem always did. As they walked towards the rounded end-cap that made-up part of the front of the restaurant, he kept his hand on the small of her back while they talked. Mir and I approached quietly. Max had come out and was keeping a discreet distance. He nodded once at us. Chantal and her date were so busy running their mouths they didn't notice us. They stopped in front of one of the huge picture windows and turned toward each other. She smiled as he thanked her and told her he had a nice time. She said something like that to him, too. And then, the nigga made the mistake of lifting her chin with his finger and leaning in to kiss her.

My brother was just a blur of movement. I know that prissy

ass nigga with Chantal didn't know what hit him, literally. In just a few seconds, Mir had that nigga on the ground and his fists were turning dude's face into a bloody mess. I almost felt sorry for him. Chantal's cry broke into my thoughts. I wasn't a language buff like the twins—they caught on to them easily and were fluent in several—but I knew enough from high school and college French to know that she was upset.

"Tamir!" she screamed. "*Oh, non!* What are you doing? Tamir, *arrête*! Stop! *S'il te plaît.* Oh, God, Tre, please." She turned her attention to me, because Mir wasn't having none of it. I looked where Max was managing to keep a crowd from gathering—nobody would approach us with his big, strapped ass standing there—down to where Mir had almost beat this nigga unconscious. Then, I looked at this girl, crying and pleading with me.

"Tre," she said, "*Ça suffit.*" *That's enough.*

I sighed. As much as I was enjoying it, I couldn't deal with crying females and Mir had proven his point. I started pulling my brother off. He resisted at first, until I threatened to punch *his* ass. I finally got him up and off the man, although he couldn't resist kicking the nigga one last time. Chantal moved toward the bloody mess that was her date. "Oh, Aiden," she said, kneeling next to him, tucking her little bag under her arm so that she could cup his face. "*Désolée... Je suis désolée.*"

Mir yanked out of my arms. "Yo, ma, you apologizing to that nigga? Get your ass up!" he pulled her up forcefully.

"Don't touch me!" she cried, trying to jerk away from him. He wasn't letting go.

"You think you gone be catering to another nigga while I'm standing here? Hell, nah. You ain't gone do that shit period."

She looked up at him and her face darkened. "You don't own me. You don't tell me what to do. *Je te hais*, Tamir!"

He didn't even respond to her saying she hated him. Instead, his voice dropped another level. "Give Tre your keys. We bout to go home." I could tell she wanted to argue, but one look at his face had her reaching in the clutch, grabbing the keys, and handing them to me.

He didn't speak to me all the way to his house. Not that I gave a fuck. I was more than used to his silence. And I didn't want to talk to him anyway after that shit he just pulled. I felt terrible for what I'd gotten Aiden into and I was going to check on him as soon as possible.

"Where's my baby?" I asked him as I walked from the detached garage to the front door of the house.

"You wasn't worried about *our* baby when you was all up in that nigga face smiling," he shot back.

"Just like you don't be worried about her when you off fucking any bitch that gaps her legs," I retorted, unlocking the door and doing my best to shut it in his face.

That didn't work, though. He caught it and pushed it open easily before walking in and slamming it behind him. I made my way toward the stairs, ready to get away from his lunatic ass. I shrieked when he grabbed me from behind and carried me back to the couch. Jumping up, I faced him with my fists on my hips. No way was I going to sit down and cower while his six-foot-four ass loomed over me.

"You really think you finna have an attitude with me about some nigga? Nah, ma. It don't work like that."

"You were so wrong for that shit! That man did nothing to you and you beat him like… like… like you some kind of savage animal! You do too fucking much," I yelled.

"He *did* do something to me. He touched something that

belongs to me. Now he knows better." He shrugged and I wished for a bat to knock him upside his nonchalant head. Instead, I paced back and forth, trying to get my temper and my words in order.

"I do *not* belong to you. Aiden is my friend and what you did out of some fucked up sense of possessiveness is horrible. You-" I paused as he approached me. I walked backwards, away from him, but he never stopped. Finally, my back met the wall and he had me cornered. He put a hand on each side of my head.

"I don't want to hear that nigga's name come out your mouth again." His voice was a low growl. "And you know damned well you belong to me." I sucked in my breath as he nuzzled my neck. "What part of you doesn't belong to me, DuBois?" He brought his hand up and placed it over my left breast. I hated how my nipple pearled against his hand immediately. I hated how I could be mad at him, be hurt by him, but want him beyond anything. "You gon lie and say what's under here don't belong to me? Your breasts that nurse *my* baby? Your heart that I know is mine?" he whispered against my lips. I tried to turn my head, but I couldn't. His minty breath washed over my mouth and I wanted him to kiss me so bad that I could cry. *No, Chantal. Stay focused!*

"Your lips don't belong to me, ma? When I can make you fall apart with a kiss? When I get you so hot that you beg to suck my dick?" I closed my eyes, refusing to acknowledge the truth of what he was saying. His hand left my breast and traveled down to brush across my stomach. "This spot right here that got big when you carried my daughter? That's mine. And your womb? I'm the only nigga who gon ever plant babies there. Any seed that grows there? *Mine*." He was seducing me with his words, his mouth on my neck, his hand stroking my body. I wanted so much to melt into him, be consumed by him, truly *belong* to him. But, I just couldn't.

And then I felt the silken slide of his hand under my dress, across my thighs…

"Tamir, *non*…" I didn't even convince myself. He smiled at me because he knew I was fronting. The smile grew as he made contact with the thoroughly soaked seat of my panties.

"No?" he taunted. "*My* pussy remembers me. Look how wet it gets for me." His fingers crept below the barrier of my panties. He gently stroked my clit and my knees almost buckled. It had been soooo long and he felt soooo good. I whimpered and couldn't help looping my arms around his neck and letting my head fall to rest against his shoulder. I almost cried when he gently eased a finger inside me. I rocked against it greedily, wanting more, wanting something else… "Look how tight *my* pussy is, DuBois. Because it's only ever felt me. Because the only dick it'll ever know is *mine*. You don't remember the ways I marked it, DuBois? The times I fucked you so hard that it was tender and swollen? The times I fucked you so much that it was full of my cum? The times-"

"Tamir, *mon coeur*, please," I begged. His words were doing things to me, overwhelming me. I felt light-headed, hot, so damned hungry as he stretched and fucked me with two of his fingers.

"Yeah, you're mine. All mine, DuBois. I'll kill another nigga before I let him have you. You understand?" I nodded helplessly, rocking my hips against his hand.

"I take care of you. I provide for you. I put this roof over your head and the keys to that Benz in your hands. I make it so you never have to worry about money again. You will not disrespect me by entertaining another fucking nigga. You are *mine*."

He may as well have dumped me in the Arctic Ocean. My eyes flew open. I pushed on his shoulders. "Move," I said. He didn't budge, so I repeated it in French. "*Bouge-toi*, Tamir!"

He stepped back and eyed me. Slowly, I worked my way out of the dress. I stood facing him in an emerald green bra and panty set. I unhooked the bra and watched him lick his lips as I let it slide down my arms. I bent to ease my panties down my legs and over my shoes. I kept my face down until I had control of my tears. When I stood up, I stared at him defiantly.

"What are you doing, DuBois?" he asked.

I shrugged one shoulder. "Offering you what you've paid for. I'm kind of flattered that I'm such an expensive piece of property. I mean the Benz and house alone, should earn you an extra sloppy blow job on top of the usual services."

He shook his head. "Nah, that's not what I meant, and you know it, shorty."

Maybe I did know it, but I was coming from a place of hurt and insecurity. I walked over to the couch and lay on it so that my feet were pointing in his direction. Slowly I pulled my legs up, then opened my thighs. I used my hands to gently part my lower lips, giving him a full view of my sex. "Well, *allez*, Tamir. Come get what you bought."

The anger that blazed across his face was frightening in its intensity. I dropped my head back, not wanting to see it, not wanting him to see my tears. Finally, after what seemed like the longest silence in history, I heard, "Fuck you, DuBois."

The front door slammed.

I fell apart.

Briar

Dinner time and I was ready. I was so glad my best friend, Dominique, wanted to meet at Pappadeaux. I been craving their Seafood Fondeaux and if she didn't hurry up, I was gone start without her. Maybe I was a little impatient. I knew Nique's practice—she was a pediatric cancer specialist—might be even busier than mine. But hell, I was hungry. I was so busy staring at the menu that it wasn't until I smelled the tell-tale fragrance of her Gucci Guilty perfume that I realized she had approached the table. I smiled up at my girl. Dominique was beautiful, her long hair pulled into a classy bun, her pretty brown skin glowing, and her model-type body draped in an off-the-shoulder blouse and slacks. She definitely didn't look like a woman who'd just broken up with her fiancé a year ago. But then, Dominique and Lucas had never really been in love and I, for one, was glad the marriage was called off. She kissed me on both cheeks, then slid into the other side of the booth.

"What's up, Buttercup?" she asked, smiling at me warmly.

To most people, Dominique came off as the original ice-princess. You'd think a smile would break her face. But with me and her patients, another part of her nature came through. I was glad we'd met and clicked at a Baylor alum event. I rolled my eyes.

"Girl! I have so much to tell you."

We were interrupted by our server and she and I quickly

ordered hurricanes—and my Fondeaux. As soon as we were alone again, I told her about the encounter in my office with Tyrese Kinsey. Her expressions let me know how crazy it all sounded and I wondered for the millionth time if I didn't let him off too easy.

Well, that wasn't exactly true. I *knew* I let him off too easy. I just wondered what that meant about me and Mr. Kinsey. Nique didn't say anything as our server brought our drinks.

"So, let me get this straight—a guy you suspect of being involved in some questionable activities broke into your office, accessed your computer, felt you up, and promised to come back… and you just let him walk away?" she asked.

Well… when you put it like that… I nodded in shame. She took a long swallow of her hurricane.

"Good. He obviously shook your ass up," she announced, before taking another sip.

I stared at my practical, by-the-book bestie in shock. "I'm sorry, what?"

She sighed, then shrugged. "Elyse, we spend all our time being good and playing by the rules and look at us. Beautiful, accomplished women sharing dinner with each other on a Friday night. Fuck it. Go for what feels good for once. If he can almost make you nut with just his words and hand, imagine if you let him get you in the bed."

I kept looking at her as if she'd sprouted another head. "You're a really beautiful clone of my best friend, but could you send her back now?"

"What you want me to say, Lyse? You've already told yourself all the problems. You know damned well you had no business letting him take off when he potentially has sensitive, confidential information. You know that you probably shouldn't be thinking about seeing him again. So what do you want me to add? I know you. You've gone through all of this in your head six million times, and yet you're still interested. So, fuck it. Go for it." She shrugged again.

I dropped my forehead into my palms. "Then, he's a baby!"

"Is he legal?" she asked.

I nodded.

"Girl, then climb on top of him and ride him into the sunset. Get it out of your system. I swear I think I could eat a whole seafood platter by myself tonight." She changed subjects as if the shit she was saying was typical for her. I'd never known Dominique to "be intimate" with anyone—she had even planned on making her fiancé wait til marriage. I don't know for sure that she was a virgin, but she was pretty damned close, something I found amazing for a woman who was so gorgeous and almost 30-years-old. She looked up from the menu into my confused face and sighed.

"Look, honey bun. If I've learned nothing else this last year, I've learned the importance of passion. Do something passionate, Lyse. Hell, let me live vicariously."

I shook my head. "Maybe," I said. "I don't wanna talk about Tyrese any more. Let's talk about this food. I'm ready to smash." I picked up my menu.

"You know, it sounds like your office would benefit from getting a security specialist like Daniel Cruz, all jokes aside."

She was just full of surprises tonight. Nique swore she hated Daniel Cruz, her ex-fiance's brother-in-law, but here she was giving him a recommendation. I narrowed my eyes. "You have something positive to say about Daniel Cruz?"

"Just because he's a rude, arrogant ho doesn't mean he's not the best at his job. He's a thorn in my side, but he knows security," she said, refusing to look at me.

"Mm-hmm. In your side, huh? You know he trying to be in your-"

"Briar Elyse Rose, don't be vulgar. It's so unbecoming," she interrupted me.

I smiled. This was the prim, proper Dr. Walsh I was used to. I shook my head and studied my menu.

"How are your parents?" Nique asked softly.

I sighed. I adored my mama and daddy and it was killing me to see them struggling through the financial and emotional difficulties that my brother's addiction caused them. He skipped bail on an attempted murder charge—none of us believed he was guilty, but still. My parents had put up their house and now they might lose it. I was working as much as I could, but between student loans and living expenses, I wasn't much help.

"They're hanging in," I said.

"Give them my love." Nique covered my hand with hers and squeezed. I blinked my suddenly tear-filled eyes.

"Girl, enough of that! Let's eat!"

TYRESE

I had to give it to Becca—she and her friend LeeAnn just might be the experts they claimed they were. I looked down as both blonde heads bobbed in my crotch, one giving me the sloppy head I loved and the other sucking and licking on my balls. Becca looked up at me as she gagged and tried to smile around my soldier. I stroked her hair as her eyes watered. "That shit good, ma," I told her. I closed my eyes and leaned back against the headboard. My mind wasted no time creating a picture to go with the soft hands and wet lips working my dick. Only, the star of my daydreams wasn't an eager little snow bunny. It was all Dr. Briar Rose, her chunky ass butt-naked and looking like a peanut-butter-colored fantasy, her fat ass lips pulling on me like she was thirsty as hell.

"You like that, Daddy?" she asked me in that soft voice.

"Hell, yeah, shorty." Swear a nigga almost moaned that shit. I did moan when she took me to the back of her throat and hummed around me. I reached down and grabbed hair—my mind pretending it was the tight spiral curls of her shoulder-length natural hair—as I fed her more of this dick. She took it like a pro and I felt my nut rising, my balls tingling and my hips moving against her face. "Shit, Briar, I'm about to-"

Three sounds intruded right then. First, the "POP" of Becca releasing my dick, then her asking me, "Who the fuck is Briar, Ty?" with much attitude. But the third was what caught my

66

attention and had my dick starting to deflate. My work phone was going off.

"Move," I ordered my bedmates. My voice must've told them how real I was because they jumped up with a quickness. I pulled on my shorts quickly and answered the phone as I sprinted down the stairs, for privacy. "Wazzam?"

"Ma said somebody was lurking around the crib. We need to check it out." I picked up on Tripp's code immediately—the crib was one of our spots in Midtown, where one of our most-trusted lieutenants—Jean-Baptiste Michel lived, and something had gone down. Saying "Ma" meant we'd meet up in River Oaks.

"Here I come," I said and hung up. I went back upstairs and dressed in under a minute, I swear. Becca and LeeAnn just watched. "Lock your door," I told them before heading out.

It didn't take me long to make it to my parents' house where my family was waiting. We gathered in Pops' soundproofed study before anyone said anything. Tre spoke first.

"We got a rat. The crib ain't even a typical trap. It ain't a bando. Hell, it's some middle-class shit. And Jean-Baptiste ain't the type to draw attention. Ain't nobody just figured that shit out."

Me and my brothers nodded in agreement. Tamar touched Tre's arm. "Who you think it is, Brother?" she asked him.

"I don't-" he stopped as his phone went off. He read the message and blew out a long breath. "Shit. We got a problem. Doc ain't there and Jean-Baptiste fucked up pretty bad."

I instantly went on alert—my brothers and I were close as hell, but we'd developed close friendships with some of our team, too. Me and Jean-Baptiste were tight like Tre and Bones. "What? He got hurt?" I asked. "Why we can't just do a hospital drop?"

"He won't go," Tripp said. "The police gone come because of the gunshots and his papers ain't right."

Shit. J.B. had been around so long I forgot he was a Haitian immigrant.

"Backup doc?" I asked.

"Ain't never needed one," Pops said. Doc had been handling our shit since Pops was running the streets. They grew up together. Doc's wife was a nurse and they worked together.

I wasn't about to let my boy suffer. "Tre, tell 'em to get into Doc's treatment room somehow. Send Bones—that nigga could get into Ft. Knox. I'll bring a doctor." Before any of them could ask, I was out the door.

I knew where she lived. I'd been looked that up, planned to surprise her one day. She was about to be surprised now, but not how I imagined. I was at her door in 20 minutes. Bad as I just wanted to go in and get her, I knocked.

And knocked.

And finally rang the doorbell. "Damn, Briar, wake your ass up, ma," I yelled.

I heard her a minute later scrambling behind the door. "Who is it?" she said, her voice sounding sexy with sleep.

"Tyrese. Open the door, shorty!" She must've thought about it, because it took a few seconds for her to crack it open and look at me. Her chain lock was still on.

"Mr. Kinsey, what the hell-"

"I need you to come with me." I didn't let her get her sentence out. Her eyes widened.

"It's almost midnight. I just worked a double in the ER. And even if I hadn't, I wouldn't go anywhere with you. I don't know you like that!"

She tried to close the door, but I already had my foot in it.

"Briar-"

"Nobody calls me that. Move your foot."

"*I* call you that. And no. I need a favor, Briar."

She rolled her eyes. "I don't give out my favors to strange men at midnight."

I made up my mind to follow up on that later, but now was not the time. "I'm not really asking, Dr. Rose," I said, lowering my voice.

"Are you threatening me? Because I swear to God this time, I *will* call the police. You go too damned far, Tyrese Kinsey! You are not above-"

Something told me to try a different way. "Briar. Please. I need you." That got her quiet. "If you don't help me, my friend is going to die. Come on, ma. What about that oath y'all take and shit? Please?"

She stood there clutching that door and peeking at me for what seemed like forever. Then she closed her eyes and sighed. I smiled.

"Fine. Let me get my clothes and some stuff. And I'm telling my best friend I'm with you, so if you plan on killing me-"

"I'ma kill that pussy later, ma, but not tonight. Can you hurry up, though?"

She shook her head and slammed the door.

I had no decent judgment where this man was concerned. None. I could not be trusted. Out at midnight riding in a car with a man I barely knew to an unknown location. My stupid ass deserved to be found in one of Houston's bayous. He finally pulled into the driveway of an upscale home in a gated community.

"Get out," he said. Hell, I had obeyed everything else. Why start objecting now? He walked around to my side of the car and grabbed my hand. Even though he was basically pulling me up the driveway, my palm against his caused me to tingle in totally inappropriate ways. The door to the house was pulled open by one of the scariest men I had ever seen in my life. He looked to be 6-foot-6 of muscle and mean, with colorful tattoos all down his arms and up his neck, a small skull and crossbones on one cheek, multiple piercings, and a mug. He smirked at me as I stepped closer to Tyrese. But all he said was, "Down the hall on the right, Ty."

"Thanks, Bones."

I followed Tyrese. To my surprise, I found what damn near amounted to a fully functional operating room, guarded by two men who gave us head nods. And on the table in the middle of the room lay another mountain of a man, his shirt and upper pant leg soaked in blood. Tyrese immediately walked to him.

"Say, nigga, why you always somewhere tryna play

Superman?" he asked. His voice was gruff, but I could hear the concern. The man smiled weakly.

"Gotta… gotta cover for… yo… weak ass. What… about Van?" he struggled to say. Tyrese looked at one of the guards. The man shook his head. I figured Van had been less fortunate.

Tyrese avoided the question. "Just lay back, bro. I brought help. But don't get fly with her," he said, touching the injured man's shoulder lightly. They both looked at me expectantly.

Oh! I am *the doctor on call here, huh?* I thought. I made my way to the table.

"What's your name?" I asked.

"Jean-Baptiste," he said with a trace of an accent.

"Jean-Baptiste, I'm Elyse. I'm going to examine you and see where you're hit and what's going on, ok?" I said, my voice immediately slipping into the reassuring, authoritative tone I used with my patients.

"You… the… prettiest doc…I done… seen," he said.

I smiled. "I try. You should see me when it's not the middle of the night."

"All that flirting finna stop, before I kick yo ass, JB," Tyrese said. He really was trying to keep his friend in good spirits. I liked that.

"Shit… not even… with… bullets in me," JB said and smiled again.

"Shh," I said. I went to wash my hands and indicated for Tyrese to do the same.

"Why?" he asked.

"You see anyone else here available to assist?" I asked.

For a minute, the color drained from his caramel complexion. "I ain't no blood and guts kind of dude."

"Well good thing he has no guts on display! Can't believe

your big gangsta ass is scared," I teased. He narrowed his eyes at me but didn't deny it.

We cut JB's clothes off and found a shot to his upper thigh—thank God it just missed his femoral artery or Tyrese would've been telling his friend goodbye—one to his shoulder and another in his right upper quadrant, near his collarbone. The shots in his leg and upper chest seemed to have been through and through. But there was no exit wound on the back of his shoulder.

The room was well stocked. I gathered supplies and the implements I needed. No way would I trust myself to operate *and* fully anesthetize a man suffering from so much blood loss, but I could at least use a local. I refused to think about what it meant that all these controlled substances and other items were available in a home office and I was using them. I loved my little old medical license and didn't even want to consider losing it. But the doctor and the woman in me just couldn't *not* help JB. I would just cuss Tyrese out later for threatening my livelihood.

I worked quickly, cleaning the wounds, removing the bullet, suturing where needed. I kept up a running monologue with JB who seemed fascinated by what I was doing. I also did it to punish Tyrese who was the loveliest shade of green as I gave graphic descriptions. Finally, I was done and JB was sleep. As I washed up, Tyrese came over and tossed a small duffel bag on the counter.

"What is it?" I asked.

"Open it."

Once I dried my hands, I did. My jaw dropped. Inside was more cash than I'd ever seen in one place. "Tyrese-"

"You saved my nigga. My friend. It's nothing, ma."

Part of me wanted to refuse the money, knowing the source

was probably questionable, but who was I fooling? This could go toward helping my parents.

Suddenly, I had an idea. *Don't do it, Elyse! This is crazy. You'll be risking everything you worked for!* But the words bubbled up, anyway. "Do you…" I cleared my throat. "Do things like this happen often?" He tilted his head to look at me.

"Why?"

I shrugged. "A side hustle never hurt anyone," I said.

He stared at me for a minute. Then, he nodded. "I got you."

(The next morning)

I sat at a table in the study with Tavion, Pops, my brothers—and my sister who was determined not to be left out. I made a steeple with my fingers and rested my chin on my thumbs.

Somebody was finna die. We lost two good men last night and almost lost JB. Plus, them niggas boosted 200 bands and the product that was there. We already needed to re-up, so this shit was extra aggy. I could feel one of my moods building and, without Shamar to calm me, I wasn't motivated to dial it back. I wanted to let it loose, just blow shit up and take niggas out. I guess my feelings showed on my face.

"You a'ight, my nigga?" Tripp asked.

I blew out a long breath. "Yeah, I just need to pop a motherfucker's eyeballs out or disembowel somebody or something," I reassured him.

They all looked at me. "What?" I said.

"Tre, most people would say they wanted to kick somebody's ass or just kill them," Pops responded.

I frowned in confusion. "That's what I said."

Tripp shook his head, but started talking. "Nobody but Pops, us brothers, a few lieutenants, and maybe Case and Bones know where the crib is located. Hell, Tay and Tavion didn't even know. I doubt that Van and Javier were the snitches—unless the motherfuckers took them out so they wouldn't come clean. And I'd put it on my life that a few others wouldn't do no ho shit like that."

"We can't think like that, bruh. Everybody suspect. Even Bones," I said, to show how serious I was. Bones was my Ace, but I couldn't even trust him right now. My family nodded reluctantly. Tripp got up and went to an old-school blackboard Pops kept in here for shit like this. He started writing names and the brainstorming about dates, locations, who might have beef, who might be getting blackmailed and other relevant shit began. Just when we had narrowed the list as far as we could right now, Shamar texted me.

MOUSE:

Please come over. We need to talk. I've made a decision.

I read the message about 15 times before replying.

ME:

I ain't for no bullshit. I already told you how it's gone be. What you feed my baby today?

MOUSE:

Tremell, this is not bullshit!

She had the nerve to put that little mad, red face next to her words.

ME:

Working, shorty. I'll be there in a minute.

MOUSE:

K

I blew out another breath. If I went over here and this girl was talking out the side of her neck, I was just gone kill everybody on Tripp's list. Fuck it. That'll solve all our problems and make me feel better.

"How's JB?" I asked Ty.

"I think he gone be all right. My doctor friend promised she'd check up on him," he said.

"I can't believe one of your hoes a doctor," Tripp said. I had to agree. Ty liked his women fast and loose and what he wanted from them didn't require too much intelligence.

"She ain't no ho, Tripp. Watch your mouth." All of us looked as that nigga clap backed. My jaw may have even dropped.

"Well, I'll be damned," Tay said. "One of 'em finally got your ass. I gotta meet this girl."

Ty mugged her. "She ain't got me. She ain't even my girl. I just-" he stopped, but we were all waiting. "Change the damned subject," he finally said.

The conversation in the room shifted to security for the block party we were having Saturday—Tavion was finally turning 18. Rather than rent out a club where his girl might be uncomfortable —she was about ready to pop with that baby—we were gone take over an abandoned lot near one of the traps. Tay had made sure it was cleaned off and mowed and I know she and mama had handled some other logistics. There was an adjacent community center that we'd rented so people could escape the heat if necessary and we could keep the food safely. Security would have to be in force though—I wasn't worried about us, but all the ladies would be there. It'd be easier to have it at our

parents' place, but the way our plans for turning up were set up…
our crowd might be too much for River Oaks.

"Listen, what y'all want me to do about this list, because I
gotta duck out for a minute?" I asked.

Pops started shaking his head. "Nothing yet. Possibility that
there's some good, loyal soldiers on there. We don't need you
making enemies out of friends. Let us work this end. You be
ready to enforce."

Shit, he ain't have to tell me twice. I saluted all of them,
hugged my mama and sister, and was out. The 20 minutes it took
me to get to Shamar's house passed by as my mind was caught
up with whatever her decision was. I parked and let myself in—
she wasn't getting that damned key back. Her salty ass wasn't in
the living room, though.

"Mouse?" I started walking toward the kitchen—seemed like
she was always eating then throwing up—but she answered from
the bedroom. She was actually propped up, all under the covers,
watching TV. I frowned at her. "What's wrong with you? You
usually fussing about how you need to get out the house. You
sick?" She shook her head. My heart dropped as I considered the
next possibility. "Something wrong with the baby?"

"No, Tremell. I'm fine. We need to talk. Sit down."

I moved to stand next to the bed, but I didn't sit down. "My
ears work with me standing up," I told her. She shrugged.

"You always want shit your way. I'm not talking until you do
what I asked," she said, her eyes going back to the TV.

I was usually a calm nigga. For real. I done even decapitated
a nigga calmly. But between the threats to my family, the hits on
our spots, her stubborn ass, and the fact that she been denying me
that pussy for over a month, I was about to blow. I snatched the
remote control out of her hand and threw it across the room

77

where it broke some shit. She started screaming some, "How dare you?" bullshit. Before she could move, I straddled her hips, careful not to touch her stomach, and pinned her hands above her head. "Look, I came like you asked. You think you finna keep playing these games with me but you not. I ain't a nigga to be played with, or-"

"Or what? What, Tremell? What you gone do?" she taunted me, twisting her wrists against my hands trying to get away.

And that was the problem. I didn't have an answer. My whole life, I got what the fuck I wanted, when the fuck I wanted it. My parents spoiled me. Bitches let me get away with murder. My victims always gave in. Even in prison, I had shit my way. But I had nothing to hold over her. Even if she wasn't carrying my seed, hurting her would be the same as hurting myself.

Fuck! Yo stupid ass done fell in love!

She looked up at me, fire shooting out of her eyes. "Get off of me!"

I was so shocked at what had just clicked in my head that I did. But nah, a nigga ain't going all the way out like that. "I don't give a fuck what yo little decision is. I told you what it's gon be. I got business to handle. I'll text you later." I turned around and started walking to the door.

"Tremell?" she called me softly.

"Fuck you want?"

"Come here for a minute."

I knew I shouldn't go back, but damn, ma got a nigga head fucked up. I turned around. She'd thrown the covers back and was kneeling on the bed. Shorty had on some little sexy black negligee shit that had her titties sitting up just right. I don't know what was going on in my head right then, but my dick was focused on getting inside her. I walked over. She knee-walked to the edge of the bed, looked at me for a minute, and then her hands started moving, down into the basketball shorts I had on. She found my dick and started stroking at the same time that she started kissing my chest. Mad as I was, I couldn't help it when my shit started growing in her hand.

"You really wanna leave without hearing?" she asked.

I pushed her ass down on the bed and climbed between her legs. Shit, I'd missed being there. I moved long enough to pull her up and take her nightie off. Freaky ass never wore no panties. She reached for me and I let her have the kiss she wanted, fighting her tongue with mine, putting a little extra pressure on her soft ass lips, letting her know I was in control. She grabbed at my t-shirt and I pulled it off. Shorty surprised me by cupping her breasts.

"Rub your chest against them," she pleaded. I did what she wanted and felt her nipples get hard as hell. Her breasts were really sensitive and pregnancy must be making it even better. I pulled back and she moaned until I slid down and took her right nipple into my mouth as I teased the other one with my fingers. Using my tongue, I tried to press it to the roof of my mouth while sucking hard. She cried my name and her fingers pulled on my hair. I released her breast long enough to look up at her. "Tell me you missed me."

"I missed you, Daddy," she whispered. Swear my dick got harder. I rewarded her by treating her left breast to the same treatment. My hand made its way down her body, to the center of her. I smiled. Baby was soaking wet and ready. I played between her lips, brushing lightly on her clit, teasing her opening with the tip of one finger.

"Tremell! Please!"

"Please, what?" I said, moving my hand to her thigh as I slid back up to meet her eyes.

"Put it back."

"Or what? What, Shamar? What you gon' do?" I used her words against her.

She didn't answer, just smiled and her hand went back into my shorts. She pumped me until I was moving helplessly against her hand. "You don't want this?" she murmured, pulling me close enough to rub my tip between her folds. My pre-cum and her juices meant I slid up and down easily. I couldn't take that shit! I didn't even have my shorts all the way down when I dived into her. My boo always felt like she was made for me, like warm, wet silk wrapped around me as tight as possible. But this? The level of heat and her juiciness was better than anything I'd ever felt. I had to stop my toes from curling as her muscles worked around me, welcoming me home. I was about to nut, no lie.

I jumped up cause a nigga wasn't about to embarrass himself. I took a minute to strip out of my shorts and let my nut settle. She whispered my name and reached for me. I climbed back into the bed and eased into her this time. Even as slow as I went, it was a struggle to keep it together. "Fuck, ma," I hissed.

She smirked at me. "Ain't no pussy like pregnant pussy, you said."

"Be quiet before I keep that belly big."

"Hell, n-"

I kissed her to cut off her words. I kinda liked that idea, could imagine shorty holding my little man's hand while her belly was round with my little mama. I moved inside her and she locked those soft thighs around me. I tried to go slow and easy, but she wasn't having it. "More, Tremell." Her fingernails dug into my arms and she insisted, "Harder."

"I don't wanna hurt the baby," I whispered.

"The baby is well-protected," she pouted. "Fuck me!"

"Nasty mouth!" I pulled all the way back.

"Shut u-" She couldn't finish the word as I slammed back into her. I could tell I took her breath. I smiled down at her and did it again. "Like that, Mouse? Huh? Is that what you want?" She didn't respond verbally. Instead, she laced her fingers through my hair and jerked my mouth down to hers. My good girl wanted it rough. After the last few weeks, I had no problem giving it to her that way. I rode her hard as she shredded my skin with her nails and bruised her lips against mine. I tangled my fingers in her hair and pulled her closer. We were sweating hard, slipping and sliding against each other, the friction adding a wet note to the sound of our bodies slapping against each other. She screamed as she came but I wasn't done. I pulled out and flipped her over and she immediately lowered her chest to the bed.

"Good girl. You know how Daddy wants it," I said, spanking her ass. I pounded into her, smacking that ass until her skin was red. I knew she liked it because, impossibly, she got wetter and worked back against me. I leaned over her back and bit her neck as I pulled her hair. "I'm finna cum." The way her pussy was working around me, I knew she was ready, too. "Milk your dick, baby."

"Tremell!" She contracted around me again and I exploded into her, my dick as far in her as possible, my fingers digging into her hips, my teeth buried in her neck. We collapsed onto the bed, and I was careful to keep most of my weight off of her.

Shamar

For a long time, the only sound in the room was our harsh breathing. He turned us onto our sides so I wouldn't be on my baby bump. Pulling me into his arms, he was ready to spoon me, but I resisted. I turned over to face him. "Tremell, I still have something to tell you."

"Lil worrisome girl! I'on wanna hear that shit right now. Go to sleep," he ordered.

"No."

"Can we at least enjoy the aftermath of our makeup sex?"

I rose up on one arm. "This was NOT makeup sex!"

He looked at me wordlessly.

"What?" I asked.

"I'm waiting on you to say something else so I can try to read your lips. Apparently, my ears ain't working." He mugged me. "Fuck you talking about, Shamar? This shit is settled. I fucked up. I'm sorry I ever entertained that bitch. I ain't tryna be with nobody but you and my seed. You-"

"Tremell, listen! FUCK! LISTEN!"

He surprised me by getting quiet. But he looked sad.

"What's wrong?"

"I feel bad because I'm about to have to have my baby committed to a mental hospital while she carrying my little one. Obviously, she done lost her damned mind, yelling at me," he said.

I rolled my eyes, but started talking. "We have the most

unorthodox relationship. We met as a result of my being kidnapped and we had sex within a week of knowing each other because everything was so intense. And then everything with your family business and this undeclared war and Katerah and the accident with Cynaa and now I'm pregnant. All within two-and-a-half months. It's so fast. Too fast."

He started shaking his head. I knew he wouldn't like where this was going. "I don't give a damn about speed. I asked you-"

"I was caught up! I'm still so caught up! I don't know, Tremell. I just-"

"I know. I FUCKING KNOW. You not leaving me. You not! I don't wanna talk no more." His eyes were darkening, looking through me. I grabbed his face.

"Don't you leave this moment, Tremell. I deserve to be heard. I think we need to slow down-"

He worked to stay with me. "We just had sex. You carrying my baby. It's too late for slow, ma. You in this with me."

"Can we talk about what I want, for once?"

He gritted his teeth but nodded.

I tried again. "I think… I think we should try to do this the right way."

"Like get married?" He shrugged and his eyes started to lighten. "You think we should get married because you're pregnant? We can get married after all this shit is over. You wanna ring? We can go get one tomorrow."

I shook my head. "That's my point. Do we know each other well enough to be married? I think… I want you to date me." He looked at me in disbelief. "I'm serious. We should date and see if we really grow to like each other, if we're compatible." He just kept looking. "Tremell! Say something."

He lay on his back and put one hand under his head. He

83

stroked his beard with the other. "You saying- I mean, all this shit is about you wanting me to take you out? You so damned young and idealistic-"

"It's not about going out. It's about building a relationship," I countered.

"What you want me to do?"

I shrugged. "If you want to win me over, you figure it out."

He smacked his lips. "Girl, I already got you. I always get what I want. I'ma date the hell out your little ass. Have you all in your chest."

I raised one eyebrow. "Don't be so sure. Maybe someone else will come along-"

He grilled me again. "Don't play. Fuck around and get a nigga killed."

"I'm serious, Tremell. Both of us should leave ourselves open to that possibility." He went absolutely still and quiet. That shit was scary. I waited for him to describe the torture waiting for anyone who stepped to me. He surprised me.

"Both of us, huh? Whatever you say, shorty." I looked at him. I knew he was lying, but I didn't know what the catch was. He betta not be considering that Katerah bitch! Of course, I couldn't say that since I'd started this.

"And, shorty? Since we starting over? No sex until we see how compatible we are, ok?"

Oh, hell, no! "You know my hormones got me super horny, Tremell!!" I whined. He *knew* how hot I stayed since I've been pregnant. He was just being an ass!

"I'm not gone let sex cloud our judgment. Thank me later."

H ow did you make a six-foot-six, 225-pound thug leave when he didn't want to?

You didn't.

I glared at Tripp as he sprawled out in my floor, coloring with Naa. Ever since baby girl had gotten better, the two of them had been practically inseparable. He took her to pre-school—she was doing a three-day-a-week kindergarten prep—and picked her up. He fixed her plate at dinner, helped her practice her sight words and simple math, and acted like he was deep in thought when she asked his opinion about what to wear to school the next day. He would stay until she fell asleep, then, no matter how (pitifully) I tried to avoid it, he'd kiss me til my bones dissolved and leave.

I was failing miserably at breaking up with him. I walked into the kitchen where the timer had just sounded and pulled the pan of yeast rolls out of the oven. I fixed three plates of homemade mashed potatoes, meat loaf, green beans, and rolls and set them on the table. "Y'all come eat!" I yelled. I had an attitude because I loved this nigga and I shouldn't. Loving him was dangerous.

And so easy, I admitted as I heard him talking softly to my daughter as they straightened up. He helped her wash her hands and they walked into the kitchen laughing.

"What's so funny?" I snapped, rolling my eyes.

Tripp grilled me. "How yo damned eyes gon get stuck like that one day, mean self."

Cynaa giggled. "Mama, you gon look silly." I couldn't help smiling down at her.

Dinner was noisy with their laughter and Cynaa's chatter, and messy as she got the meatloaf topping all over her mouth. Tripp's hand kept going under the table and stroking along my inner thigh. I stepped on his foot repeatedly and he acted like it didn't bother him. He drew various shapes with just the tips of his fingers along my highly sensitive skin. He'd circle his way to the edge of my panties and then draw back. Despite my irritation, I was hot and wet for him. He gave me an innocent look.

"Sure you feel okay, Cyn?" he asked. I glared at him because I didn't trust my voice.

Cynaa let out a big yawn, then. Tripp and I jumped into action. He cleaned the kitchen while I helped her bathe and get ready for bed. The two of them picked out her outfit and she settled beneath the covers. Before he could finish reading the story she chose, she was asleep. We left her with her door open and night light on.

"I'll be by to get her in the morning," he said.

"Oh! You don't have to. I got notice that Bright Heart Kindergarten has an opening and they're considering our application. I have an interview in the morning, so I can drop her on the way."

"What time do we have to be there?"

My head snapped back as I looked at him. "Tristan, you are *not* going." He smirked at me as he chewed on his toothpick.

"Cyn Claire, I *am* going. What time?"

Oh my God, I could just imagine him strolling in, in his slow motion fashion, tats on display, grill in place, mugging the principal. I shook my head at the thought. "Tripp-"

"If they ain't got good security and I don't like 'em she ain't going!'"

"Ugh!" I knew this was going to be useless. "Tristan, Aaron is going to be there! I don't want any trouble. This would mean so much. It's the best kindergarten center in Houston!"

"Why you acting like I ain't got no home training, Cyn? You know I care about that baby's education. I care about her safety, too. Ain't no use in you enrolling her in some place that I'ma just have to take her out of!"

Seemed like I should probably remind him that he had no legal standing to take her out of school or do anything else, but I knew that would just send him off into a fit. See, that's the other thing. Even though Tripp's work put us in danger, I knew he loved us, would go to war for us. I had craved that kind of love for so long, that the thought of letting him go killed something inside me. I sighed. "Eight-thirty, Tripp."

"What time you want me to pick you up?"

I didn't even argue. "Ten til," I said, turning to walk away.

"Don't even try it," he caught me and pulled me back against him. I sighed as he dropped kisses all along the nape of my neck. That shit felt soooo good. I let him turn me around.

"Give me my sugar, Cyn-Ful," he whispered, pressing his lips against mine. He didn't go any further. I knew he was leaving it up to me.

God. I couldn't help it. I looped my arms around his neck and opened my lips beneath his.

Tristan

My baby was going to kindergarten! I had this big ol' grin that wanted to come out, but the thug in me couldn't let that happen. I was dressed down in a polo and khakis. Cyn was excited about this opportunity for baby girl, so I wanted to make it happen. I scooped them up at 7:48. She just rolled her eyes, as usual. We dropped baby off and went on to the interview.

Cynaa's sperm donor was already there when we made it. I grilled that nigga and his yella ass got even lighter. Cyn rolled her eyes at me, but I didn't give a damn. I spent way more time with my baby than he did. His stupid ass was missing out. I could tell by his tight ass mouth that he was tripping about me being there with Cyn, but I was tryna be a family man. I smiled at him.

They called the parents of Cynaa Monroe back. We walked into a room and sat in the chairs in front of a desk, ignoring each other completely until the principal came. I relaxed into my seat as I recognized her. She had her head down as she read over some basic shit about Cynaa's identifying information. But then she looked up.

And it was on! A big ol' kool-aid grin spread across her face when she saw me. Cyn narrowed her eyes and looked at me as I smiled back. "Good morning, Mrs. Castleberry."

"Mr. Kinsey! What a pleasure. I didn't realize Cynaa was your daughter!" She shook my hand as Aaron coughed.

"Well, soon to be step-daughter," I corrected. Cyn and Aaron both mugged me as we all sat down.

I smiled harder. "How is Josh enjoying the car?"

"He loves it! Thank you so much for your help choosing it!"

"We aim to please at Kinsey's."

"I've never had the owner of the dealership be so attentive, though. That's good business."

I shrugged as she complimented me. "Just doing what my pops taught me." Cyn was looking at me like I'd grown another head. I'd told her ass I had a business degree. I guess she thought I wasn't doing anything with it.

Before Mrs. Castleberry could say anything else, another lady came in. The principal introduced her as one of the kindergarten teachers who would help do the interview. She clapped once, then said, "Let's get going." I sat back as she asked Cyn and Aaron why they wanted Naa to attend here, how they planned to be involved, and questions about baby girl's "disposition." Aaron's deadbeat ass didn't have much to say, but my girl's face glowed as she described my ladybug. He finally spoke up. "She can be a little hyper-"

I mugged that bitch. "I wouldn't say hyper. She's…" I looked for the right word. "*Vibrant*. She just excited about life. Every day with her is an adventure. She-" I stopped as I realized maybe I shouldn't be talking. But all the women in the room were smiling at me and Cyn reached out to squeeze my hand and hold it. I smirked at Aaron and sat back. The interview wrapped up a few minutes later. I took the moment to ask my questions about security. Mrs. Castleberry understood where I was coming from —a lot of rich kids and politicians' kids went there. She didn't need to know about my exact need for security. By the time we finished talking, I felt like the school had its shit in order.

I wasn't worried about no interview. My little bit would be here in the fall if Cyn wanted. I winked at Cyn as Mrs. Castleberry hugged me.

Tamir

I missed my baby. Three days and I wanted to see those two little teeth and watch her creeping along her belly. I was scared I was going to miss her start crawling.

I missed her crazy ass mama, too. Bad as I wanted to hate DuBois, hell, much as I *should* hate her, I couldn't. No doubt she was a good mama to my baby. She had my house in order. And she was so goddamned fine.

I turned my key in the lock and walked into the house. Strolling through the foyer, I found myself in the living room. DuBois and Noah were cuddled on the couch, watching some children's show. I just looked at them for a minute. My ladies. *My loves.*

And then she spoke. "Where have you been, Tamir?" Her voice was flat and dry. She didn't look up at me, didn't move. Did she even really care?

"Is that your business?" I asked, lifting Noah from her arms to kiss on her. I went and sat on the love seat to catch up with my baby. DuBois didn't speak again until the little puppy show went off.

"You brought me here, away from my own world, and you treat me like shit. I'm not supposed to see anyone else, but you disappear for three days, laying up with God knows who, while I'm in a house, scared for my life." Her voice was so low I could barely hear her, at first.

"DuBois, you can dead that shit about another nigga. I

already told you that. But you're free to move around. You just gotta let my people know-"

"I'm leaving. I can't live like this. School starts back in a few weeks. I can't put my life on hold because you're in some drug war. I'on know who you think gone lay up here single and lonely while you entertaining every Meka, Keisha, and DARIA in the city!" By this point, she was yelling and she'd stood up from the couch.

I shrugged. "Take your ass on. You not taking my daughter, though."

"She's still nursing. You can't take care of her on your own! You just stayed away from her for three days."

Again, I shrugged. "I'on have shit else to say. You free to go. Noah stays. You try to take her and I'ma always come for her." For *them*. I'd always come for *them*. But I wasn't about to say that. I watched as her hands balled into fist.

"*Je te hais*, Tamir!"

I rolled my eyes. "You hate me. I know. You've said that."

"All you think about is yourself! What about me? What about my life? What about-" She stopped as tears started rolling down her cheeks. And then she started crying for real. So hard that her shoulders shook, and she was sobbing out loud.

She might as well have stuck her hand in my chest and pulled my heart out. Her tears, man. I'd never been able to take them. Probably never would. I set the baby down in her playpen and made sure she had a toy. And then I walked over to DuBois and grabbed her shoulders.

"Don't do that, ma. You gone upset the baby," I whispered to her. Swear she cried harder. I didn't know what else to do, so I pulled her in my arms. She fought me at first, but I was way stronger than her little stubborn ass. "Shh. You gon be sick, DuBois. Stop." But she must've been holding that shit in. I swung her up in my arms and went back to the couch. I just held her in my lap. "DuBois, c'mon, shorty. You know I can take anything but you crying. Shit, cuss me out or some shit, my beautiful, brown baby. Don't do this, though." Man, she had me begging, because I was finna start crying with her. I knew I was the one hurting her but I didn't know how to stop. "Tell me what you want. I'll make it happen. You been walking around here so sad and quiet and now you crying. That ain't you, ma. What you want me to do?" My voice was as soft as I could make it. I could try to get over being mad, if it would help her stop hurting. I lifted her chin and wiped her face with my hand. She tried to duck her head again, but I wouldn't let her. "Stop," I said, kissing her on her wet cheek. "Talk to me."

She was quiet for another minute. And then she took a deep breath. "You been with that bitch?"

I frowned. "Who?"

She rolled her eyes. "Your other baby mama."

I grasped her face again, made her meet my eyes. "I ain't got another baby mama. Don't plan on having one."

"You know who I mean."

"I ain't seen that girl in months," I told her truthfully.

She sniffed and finally looked at me on her own. "For real?"

"Yeah, ma." I smiled. "Why? You sound jealous."

She shrugged. "Tell me where you been." I looked at her for a minute. She started getting up off my lap. I pulled her back down.

"Chill, girl. I been at my parents'. Call Mama. She been fussing at me for not coming home."

"You didn't have to leave like that," she said, pouting.

I looked at her in disbelief. "Girl, you implied I was treating you like a prostitute! I ain't never disrespected you like that."

"Then don't bring up what you buy for me."

I leaned back against the couch. "I mean... I wasn't tryna say shit like that. I know your parents got a little dough, so it makes me—you don't understand--" I stopped and closed my eyes. I felt her touch my face.

"Tell me."

"I'm a man. It means something to me to be able to take care of you and my little mama. Like, my Pops got our back, but for Tay and Mama... it's something different."

She didn't say anything, but she relaxed against me.

"What you want me to do, shorty?" I asked her again.

"Stop leaving us. Stop being so mad."

I sighed. "I can stop leaving. But I can't promise that other one yet. My mind ain't right since the shooting. And I do get mad when I think about how I should've been there when my baby came into this world."

"I wanted you there," her voice was soft.

"I want you here," I admitted. "I don't want you to leave. I just be... You just make me so mad when you say you hate me or you don't wanna be around me." She nodded.

"Mir... What we gon do?"

"I don't know, DuBois," I said tightening my arms around her. "I don't know."

Shamar

Date night! I'm so glad Tremell took me seriously. Although, good as he looked in his button-down shirt and slacks, I kinda wanted to stay home and do him. My baby looked good on his GQ shit. Even I could tell that his clothes were tailored just for him. As for me, my pregnant self had become Devyn's and Cyn's personal fashion doll. They had me in a strapless, black, wide-legged jumpsuit. With it, I wore the yellow diamond jewelry Tremell had given me. We were on our way to a play, then dinner, but first, I had to run something by him.

"My TeTe Amber called me," I began. He tried to look innocent.

"Did? What she say? I know you were glad to hear from her," he said, playing with one of the figurines on my sofa table. "Did I tell you how pretty you look?"

I crossed my arms over my breasts. "She apologized for not being in touch and explained to me how happy she was."

Tremell raised his eyebrows. "Wow! That's good. All this time you been assuming she miserable. Look at God." He lifted both his hands like he was giving thanks.

I rolled my eyes at him. "She also knew I was pregnant somehow."

"Well, y'all *are* family. Maybe she felt that."

I popped his arm. "You ain't slick."

He pulled me against him and kissed my neck. "I fuck-up enough on my own. I ain't paying for her fuck-ups, too."

"Meddling ass," I murmured, winding my arms around his neck. He kissed me again and then slapped my ass.

"Let's go."

(*Three hours later*)

I was so damn pissed at Tremell! His ass fell asleep during the play. Here I was, talking excitedly to him, when I realized the gentleman in front of me was giving me sympathetic glances, while looking to my right and shaking his head. I turned and Tremell was sound asleep, with his mouth slightly open. As I looked back at the older gentleman, he mouthed, "You can do better."

At this point, my face was heated from the embarrassment I felt. I turned back towards the stage, no longer excited.

As the crowd surged to its feet and the lights came up, Tre stretched and asked me was I ready to go. The man in front of us mugged him and shook his head.

Tremell grilled him back. "What, old man? Betta turn yo ass around and proceed toward an exit."

The man turned up his nose. "The play would've been infinitely more enjoyable were it not for your snoring, young man!" he said with a British accent.

Oh, shit.

"How much would you enjoy it dead?" Tremell growled. That poor old fellow got pale as a ghost then damn near ran out. I turned to walk away from Tre, refusing to respond to any of his shenanigans.

"Shamar!"

I kept walking.

"Shamar!" he yelled louder.

As people begin to glance our way, I tried to calm my anger. I stopped walking, letting him catch up to me.

"What the fuck is wrong with you? I spent good money for tickets to this boring ass shit and you just gone up and walk away?"

I turned towards him with tears in my eyes and said, "You have no idea how hurt I am right now. Bring your ass on, Tremell. Let's go."

When we got to the car, Tremell stopped in front of my door and grabbed my hand. "Mouse, I fell asleep. I didn't cuss nobody out. I didn't beat nobody's ass. I didn't kill nobody." This nigga sounded genuinely confused. Smh. "I. Fell. The. Fuck. Asleep. Obviously, I wish that I hadn't, but you know a lot of shit been going on and I'm tired. Please give me another shot with dinner. I won't fuck up this part of the date."

He smiled at me and I damned near melted. Part of me wanted to tell Tremell to kiss my ass. But the part of me that loved him so hard and wanted him to be exactly what I needed, said, "Tremell, don't mess this up, please!"

In the car, I reminded him the point of our dates was to spend time together, learn more about what we had in common. How could we do that if he was uninterested and asleep? True, I picked the play, but he chose the restaurant. We were going to try out a somewhat, upscale spot called "Ambrosia." Tremell said the food was good as hell and the service was excellent. His friend owned it. Upon our arrival, we were immediately ushered past those waiting, and seated at a table. As I looked around the plush surroundings, I found myself impressed with its elegance. The waiter presented us with our menus.

"May I please have a glass of water with lemon, no ice?" I asked.

"Yes ma'am, you certainly may. May I say, you look beautiful tonight, madame?"

Tremell smirked at the waiter and said, "No, you may not. She asked for water, not drool."

The waiter hurried away and I turned to Tremell.

"Must you cause chaos everywhere we go?" I mugged him.

"Mouse, his disrespectful ass better be glad I didn't knock him out for staring at your tits. Now, I said I'd date you. I ain't never say, I'd allow anyone to disrespect me or my girl. Stop tryna turn me into somebody I ain't. And stop tryna look hard. You just look like an aggravated doll."

I looked in his eyes, took a deep breath, and looked down at my menu to keep from smiling.

"Here you are, ma'am," the waiter stated as he approached our table.

I looked up from my menu to tell him, "Thank you," and realized that he was indeed staring at my chest. Tremell noticed at the same time.

"Yo, nigga, you gone stop staring at my girl!"

At being caught gaping, the server's hands began to shake. The water slipped from his grasp and crashed onto the table, soaking the entire front of my top. I screamed because it was cold.

Tremell immediately jumped up, and with one punch, knocked our waiter to the floor, unconscious.

"Tremell!" I hissed, while jumping up. "It was an accident."

"Bitch been disrespecting me since he walked up."

The entire restaurant fell silent as management approached our table. Tremell looked around, frowning at the other diners.

"What? Y'all can get it, too!"

You should've seen them, turning back to their conversations and picking up their forks and knives. Scary asses.

The manager's voice was shaky as he started speaking. "Mr. Kinsey, you are a valued customer of this establishment, but we do not tolerate violence. I'm going to have to ask you and your dinner guest, to leave."

Tre frowned. "I ain't gotta go nowhere. Call Malcolm Weathers, the owner, and see what he says."

I shook my head. "I'm ready to go," I whispered. "Let's just go." As I gathered my purse, I don't know what was wetter, my top or my face.

This date had been an utter, complete failure.

TYRESE

Briar had that good ergonomic chair in her office. I spun around in it like I was five-years-old. She oughta be getting ready to come in for her lunch break in a minute. I did some research and found out she liked the gyros and Greek salad from Niko Niko's. I came bearing gifts. I sat back as she unlocked the door. She gasped when she saw me, then shook her head and closed the door.

"Shorty, you gotta start screaming loud when people break in on you!" I fussed at her.

"Mr. Kinsey, you have to stop breaking in and popping up on me," she said, slamming a folder down on her desk. "Why are you here?" She put that fat ass on the desk next to me and crossed her arms over her chest. She looked too cute in her white jacket. I reached down beneath her desk and pulled out my package. Her eyes widened when she saw the big-bellied dude on the front of the plastic bag.

"Niko Niko's? How did you know???" she asked, smiling and grabbing for the bag.

"Uh-uh, Dr. Rose. You hurt my feelings," I teased her.

"I'm sorry! Come on, man, before it gets colder!" She grabbed again. I moved it.

"Say please."

She pouted. "Please. Ugh!"

I shook my head. "Ol' bad ass attitude," I said, standing up. I moved in front of her. "Give me a kiss."

She glared at me. "Nope."

"Nope? Nope?! You gone give up this delicious mix of lamb and beef?"

"Yes!" But she looked doubtful.

"With this creamy tzatziki and crisp red onions?" She licked her lips. This time, when she said, "Yes," it was real unsure.

"Did I mention the Greek salad? The dressing is-" She cut me off by pressing those soft lips into mine. She tasted like strawberries and mint. Who would've thought I was gon end up with a doctor? Cause Briar Rose was definitely about to be mine. She pulled back and I half-smiled. "I forgive you," I said, handing her the bag. She slid back to sit on her desk as I sank down into the chair. "You think we could have lunch together?" I asked her. She just nodded and gestured toward the bag. She was so busy thanking me for the food and moaning over it that she didn't even notice that I had moved my chair directly in front of her. In fact, she was halfway into a bite of the first gyro and I had slipped my hands under her skirt, before her eyes flew to mine.

"Mr. Kinsey!"

"Dr. Rose," I stood up and buried my lips against her neck. Swear she couldn't help it. Her head dropped back. Her pulse pounded against my lips. "You taste so good. So sweet. And I'm hungry."

"T-T-Tyrese. No. We... I don't even..." I pulled back a little to look at her. She clutched the sandwich with both hands and those big eyes were glued to my face. I saw surprise in them.

And desire. I smiled and leaned forward to kiss her neck again.

I moved my hands up to the edge of her panties, then stroked down to her knees. Over and over, I rubbed her from the top of her thighs to her knees. Her body shifted, softening, her legs parting a little. I reached for the sides of her panties and started pulling. "I wanna see if you taste like that everywhere."

"I…"

"Eat your lunch," I told her, as I slid her panties down her legs.

Eat your lunch. He must be crazy. No way could I think about food. Hell, no way could I think as I sat on my desk, panty-less, my skirt being pushed slowly up my thighs. I set the gyro down. He gave me that slightly-crooked-but-perfect-smile that got my panties wet. Well—it would have if I had any on.

"Just lay back, Briar Rose. I got this."

No, I said. *This is my workplace. What if there's an emergency? I don't even remember if I locked the door. And I barely know you.*

Problem was, I said all that in my head as I lay back on the desk. He pulled me to the edge and pushed my skirt the rest of the way up. I felt the rush of cool air against my wetness as he parted my thighs. "Pretty," he said, and I felt my face grow warm with pleasure—like I'd been wanting his approval and didn't even know it. Tyrese kissed my inner thighs, the left one, then the right.

"Briar?" He said my name with his mouth pressed against my skin.

It took me a minute to find my voice. Finally, I squeaked out a, "Huh?"

"Want me to stop?"

He was putting the decision in my hands. And even though I knew being around this man made my ability to make decisions suspect, I loved that. Fuck it, I was a grown woman and I wanted his mouth on me more than I wanted my next breath. "No, Tyrese." I felt his smile against my thigh. He let my anticipation build as he just stroked my thighs softly with his hands and pressed kisses against them. I wiggled against him, burning up from his touch.

"Patience, young grasshopper!" he teased.

Finally, his lips discovered the top of my mound. He gifted me with open-mouthed, wet kisses there, before easing down, nibbling and sucking my lower lips. My body was shameless. I know a flood of juices met him and my knees fell open. With the very tip of his tongue, he stroked across my clit. I closed my eyes as my back arched off the desk.

"You so sensitive. I love that, ma," he whispered. He spread me with his fingers and let his mouth go to work. His teeth, his tongue, his lips… *oh my God, I'm going to die.* Tyrese swirled his tongue into shapes I didn't even know existed as he loved on my clit and my soaking wet opening. He'd bite me gently then soothe the bite with a rub from his lips or a lash from his tongue. I couldn't help the moans escaping me. At that moment, the hospital director could've walked in and he would've had to wait to fire me until I got my nut. My fingers destroyed the bun he'd pulled his locks into and I probably busted his eardrums as hard as I clapped my thighs against his ears. Still, he didn't stop.

I felt the tell-tale tremors in my lower body and stomach that let me know I was close. I tried, feebly, to push his head away, but he locked me down. He focused on my clit, licking it with more and more pressure until I thought I would explode. And then, he bit down and sucked it into his mouth as he inserted two fingers in my pussy.

I'm surprised I didn't knock every damned thing off my desk, the way my ass thrashed around as I came. It was the most intense orgasm I ever had, almost painful because Tyrese wouldn't let it end as he sucked and fucked me with his fingers. "Tyrese... *please.*" He ignored me at first and I was too weak to even attempt to push his head away. Just when I thought I was going to pass out, he sat back. My body went completely boneless as he smoothed my skirt back down. Even though I lay there for a full minute, when I stood up, I stumbled. He laughed at me and gave me the chair. I watched silently as he crossed to the door.

"Don't make plans for tomorrow night, Fairytale Girl," he said. He opened the door, then closed it again. "Oh, yeah. Sweet everywhere, Briar Rose. My new favorite dessert. I had to take a souvenir." He waved my black panties at me. Before I could say anything, he was gone. I dropped my forehead to my desk.

After work, I spent a quiet evening at home with a bottle of wine and my e-books on my iPad, snuggled up in my bed. I had to get this thing with Tyrese Kinsey under control. A casual affair was one thing, but I already knew he had the power to have me in my feelings. A relationship with him was totally unacceptable. I had too much to lose. I repeated that to myself until I fell asleep.

The next morning, I woke up feeling pretty good. I was off today, so it was time to catch up on cleaning and grocery shopping. I sat up and stretched. In the middle of a deep yawn, I heard someone banging on the door. *Who the hell...* Seconds later, the banging was joined by nonstop ringing of the bell. A male voice hollered my first name as I was bumbling my way down the stairs, trying to put on my robe. After undoing my locks, I yanked the door open.

"Tyrese Kinsey, what the hell?"

"Rise and shine, cupcake!" he said. "I brought doughnuts!"

He held up a Krispy Kreme box. I snatched it. "You gon ruin all my efforts to be slim-fine," I complained around a mouthful of glazed doughnut as I led him into my kitchen.

"Chill. You already thick-fine. You don't need to lose no weight."

I felt my skin grow warm from a blush at his compliment. "Well, thank you. What are you doing here?" I asked as I got saucers for both of us and started my coffeemaker.

He shook his head. "Rude ass. I didn't tell you about the plans for tonight. We going to a party."

I set my doughnut down on the plate. "About that."

He gave me the side eye as he grabbed a chocolate iced one. "What 'about that'?" he asked.

"Tyrese, we have undeniable chemistry. And I know we're going to end up in bed-"

He smirked. "Shit, we can go right now if you want."

"But… our worlds are so different. From the situation with JB to your clothes and your vehicle, I get the feeling that you're involved in some things that may not be good for my career."

Tyrese narrowed his eyes. "So what you saying, Briar?"

I sighed. "I don't think we should go out together."

He gave me a hard look. "Run that shit by me again?"

"Ty, I have so much to lose-"

"Let me get this straight. Not only do you want to work for me secretly, you want to fuck me in secret?"

TYRESE

ow, in any other situation, this might be a dream come true. I mean, I'd been a side nigga before, banging chicks with husbands and boyfriends. But they always ended up clingy and wanting to leave their men for me. I hated when they forgot the rules of this game. But Dr. Rose wanted something like that and I was ready to go off on her ass. I had plans for her to be my ol' lady and she up here saying shit that was finna make me pull a Tre on her.

"So now you too good for me? You wasn't when you had them thick ass thighs spread all under my mouth on your desk!" It was a low blow, but shit.

She blushed. "That is unnecessary. And it's not about being too good for you. Ty, do you realize what I did for JB could lose me my license? What if you got in trouble and we were in a relationship? The cops could follow you here and ruin any chance I have of achieving my goals. I've worked too hard and I owe too much to my parents *and* myself. Put yourself in my shoes."

I wasn't in no mood to consider her perspective. Her bougie ass didn't think I was worth the risk? Didn't wanna be my ride or die? Fuck it. I shrugged.

"You want your back banged out? I can put you in the rotation, ma," I told her.

"You don't have to be so crude," she whispered.

"Just let me know when you ready. I gotta go handle some shit before tonight. Here," he handed me his phone. "Save your number. Maybe I won't have to pop up on you again." She did as I asked. I texted her so she'd have mine.

"You want coffee?" she offered.

I shook my head. "I'm out, ma."

My mind was busy as I pushed my Aventador Roadster across the city. I had almost defended myself and my lifestyle to Briar. I'ma tell y'all something that my brothers ain't really taken the time to discuss. We been so focused on talking about our street side, that you don't know the other part of our lives. Yeah, my Pops made the beginnings of his money in the game. He's a born hustler. But he also got business sense. We owned car dealerships, an advertising firm, a popular cleaning service, a luxury bed-and-breakfast, two salons and three barbershops, Pops also flipped houses, and Mama was a realtor for upscale properties. They were looking into starting a restaurant in hopes of building a fancy chain. That's just the shit I can list off the top of my head. And even though my siblings and I balled out of control, my parents insisted all of us get an education. Tripp and Tre already had their Bachelors and I know once shit settled down, they were thinking about Masters. I was a year away from my biochemistry degree and I wanted to be a pharmacist--no drugs jokes. The twins were approaching their senior year.

Once the first degree was completed, my parents allowed us to run the business of our choice. Tripp was over one of the dealerships and, after his time at Huntsville, Tre wanted to manage a couple of the barbershops. He was sure with the presence of the Rockets, Texans, and Astros in the city, plus all the oil money, we had the opportunity to become barbers to the stars. So, nah. My life wasn't all about hustling. My parents were grooming us to eventually leave that world behind. But Briar's judgment rubbed me the wrong way. It was her loss.

But part of me felt like it was mine, too.

Shamar

I stood patiently as Devyn and Cyn made sure they were happy with outcome of the dress I'd chosen and they'd altered for me for Tavi's party. It had started out as a pretty yellow summer dress with an empire waist to make room for my growing bump. Devyn took one look at it and said, "You not wearing that Easter dress." Cyn decided it had some potential. She and Dev removed the sleeves, shortened the length—"Bitch, your legs ain't pregnant," Cyn had said—and did something with the neckline and bodice that had my breasts standing at attention. I had some nice wooden jewelry that matched the color of the espadrilles I wore. My hair was done up in a bun and bangs.

"Well???" I prompted. They looked at each other then back at me. Suddenly, I was worried. Maybe I didn't look as cute as I thought.

"Tre would kick our asses if he knew we were behind this," Cyn said, slapping Dev a high five.

"Girl, you look so good, I wanna be stereotypically gay and snap or some shit," He added. I noticed that even though he wasn't tryna be stereotypically gay, he didn't mind giving me several air kisses. *This dude.* We were in my bedroom and I started straightening a little of the mess we'd made getting ready as Cyn and Dev finished up. My besties were flawless as usual. Cyn had a spiral curl sew-in. It was black with a few orange highlights and a perfect complement to her Versace dress with its orange flowers on a black background. Block party or not, Cyn was always gon be in heels and she had on some simple-but-cute Jonatina red bottoms. Devyn wore denim pants, cuffed above his ankles, a Gucci t-shirt that featured Donald Duck, and some designer loafers.

"Y'all wanna take the Bentley?" I knew Dev loved to drive it. He surprised me though.

"Uh-uh. We going in my car," he said with a mysterious smile. Cyn and I looked at each other.

"What you up to, nigga?" she asked, giving him the side-eye.

"Just come on, tricks." We followed him out of the house. I first saw Cyn's new Platinum Edition Cayenne—it was her "mommy" car. But behind it was a bad ass Rolls.

"You bishes ain't the only ones with balling boyfriends. I told mine I was feeling neglected compared to y'all."

"And he got you a damned Rolls Royce Dawn?! Damn!" Cyn said.

Devyn waved it off. "You know I'm a Sugarbaby. Girl, the thought of losing these goodies gives that nigga nightmares." We were all laughing as we climbed in.

We talked for a few minutes about Cyn and Dev's upcoming last semester of school and then Cyn sighed.

"What, Cyn-Cyn?"

"I'm ready to party, but you know bitches gone try it and I'm not in the mood. Ugh!" She said, a frown appearing on her pretty face.

"Y'all out here looking like Bill Gates's bank account and people knowing y'all had some rocky times lately? Shiiiiit. Bitches finna try you like you on the clearance rack at Ross."

"They gone end up pressed," Cyn muttered.

I cleared my throat. "I don't know, y'all. I think Tremell and I reached an agreement that we could entertain other people. DEVYN, WATCH WHERE YOU'RE GOING!" I screamed as he swerved over the center line after I made my announcement.

"Bitch, you saying ridiculous shit about to make me wreck my car! My Sugar Daddy ain't gone like that!"

"You talking about Tremell Kinsey?" Cyn asked from the back. I nodded.

"Tremell *Nicholas* Kinsey?" Devyn added. I rolled my eyes at him.

"Was he there when y'all reached this agreement?"

"Yes, Devyn."

"And he was awake?" Cyn sounded doubtful. I turned around so she could get the eye roll.

"Hmmph," Dev said as he pulled into the lot the Kinseys had reserved for parking. "Let's see how that shit works in real life."

I could see the crowd that had already gathered near the community center and the adjacent lot. I smiled as Ced opened my door; he was always close by. He and Austin escorted us up the block. Right in the middle of the community center's yard, three of the Kinsey brothers stood holding court. I recognized that Tripp and Mir looked handsome, but I couldn't take my eyes off Tremell. It was a block party, so he was dressed simply, although I knew it all bore designer labels. He rocked all white— t-shirt, jeans, and sneakers. He had his platinum and diamond grill in and that shit was hot. His line-up was fresh, but his curls looked naughty—like someone had been running her hands through them. That shit pissed me off. I felt the mug on my face and he had one for me as he checked out my dress. I crossed my arms over my chest as he walked to me.

"Hey, ol' hot ass girl. You need to put them titties up!"

"Tremell, don't start. You usually like me in yellow. Where is Tavi?"

He ignored me. "I'm finna find you a shirt. A long one," he said, pulling at the hem of my dress.

"Boy, stop." I looked over to where Cyn was trying to keep Tripp from hugging her, then to where Devyn was talking to a couple of people. "Cyn? You wanna go in the building?" She nodded and called for Devyn. I moved to walk toward them but Tremell caught my wrist.

"Shamar, I wish you would walk off while I'm talking to you."

"Watch me, Tremell, cuz you ain't talking about nothing!" I yanked my wrist away.

"Girl!"

"Chill, Tre! It's too early for that shit," Tamir said, stepping between us. "Shay, Tavi and his girl inside."

"Thanks, Mir. I'm glad *somebody* shows the home training I know your parents gave y'all." I frowned up at Tremell.

"I know that's right," Cyn said from behind me. I knew that was directed at Tripp.

"Cyn Claire, take your mean ass on in there," Tripp said. Unlike Tremell, he seemed completely unbothered.

"Fuck you, Tristan," she said, flipping him off. He laughed.

Tremell didn't say another word to me, just looked at me with cold black eyes. I almost ran inside the center. The multipurpose room was packed, but we finally found Tavi, standing next to Anika's round self where she sat in a chair. I hugged him, said, "Happy Birthday," then dropped a kiss on Ni-Ni's forehead. "Five more weeks, mama," I told her.

"Girl! I am so ready," she said, but she was smiling.

"You being careful?"

"Yeah. I'ma leave in a minute. Just wanted to spend part of my boo's party with him. And make sure these hoes are reminded he got a family at home."

"No worries," Cyn told her. "While you two out of commission, me and Dev will be handling all hoes, bitches, tricks, and pitiful wannabe side chicks."

Devyn smiled at her in admiration. "Cyn Murray! You almost made a curse word poem!"

She shrugged. "I'm multitalented like that."

I shook my head.

"I need a selfie with the birthday boy. My public awaits," Cyn said, moving to stand by Tavi.

"Ugh, Cyn! You betta not get my fat ass in the pics," Ni-Ni said. But that girl was gorgeous and glowing, so Cyn ignored her.

Over the next hour, I swear the crowd tripled. Tamar and Mir's baby mama, Chantal, showed up—being around them and Cyn made me feel like I was in the middle of a runway show. All of them were at least five-eight, plus they wore heels. I felt like a shrimp, but a cute one. We stayed mostly on the inside because the Kinseys wanted to make sure we were safe. I knew my detail was checking in with Tremell, even though I had barely seen him since earlier. I had to admit, the party was live. Especially with a slightly buzzed Devyn and Cyn entertaining us as I bounced a little to a Migos track. I loved my BFFs.

"Outside for a little air?" Dev asked. We agreed and I called Ced and Austin over.

We made the trip outside and walked around. Cyn kept getting stopped, but the guards would only let people so close.

Suddenly, I heard Cyn say, "Not today, Satan." I looked up. Several yards away, Tripp was in a folding chair with some skank all in his lap. She whispered in his ear and then helped herself to whatever was in his cup before starting to give him a lap dance to the beat of the Future joint the outside DJ was bumping.

Cyn handed me her earrings and Tay her shoes. And then, she was gone.

"Shit," Dev said, just before he and Austin took off after her. The rest of us followed more slowly. The Lord must be working with my bestie, because she didn't drag the bitch immediately. Instead, she told her, "You need to get your stank ass up."

The girl smirked at her. "Why? Y'all broke up and I don't see no rings on him anyway. He ain't objecting so you need to get on." She leaned back against a grinning Tripp. "Sorry, Boo. This is no longer your man."

"Oh, shit," Tamar whispered.

I watched Cyn's hands curl into fists. Devyn grabbed her.

"Umm, *sorry, boo*, but I don't give a fuck what you hear in the streets. It don't matter what me and him got going, ain't nobody else stepping to him. Devyn, let me go, cuz I'm finna show this tramp."

Devyn ignored her.

Cyn's eyes flew to Tripp. "I know you better make this ho get up!"

Tripp calmly chewed on a straw. "She said she heard I'm not your man. Am I your man, Cyn Claire?"

All of us knew Tripp was drawing a line in the sand with her. They'd been going back and forth for weeks. He was about to make Cyn take a stand. Her eyes narrowed and her hands balled up even tighter. Finally, she said, "Yes, you're my man." Her voice was low, but we all heard her. Devyn let her go.

Tripp looked at the girl in his lap. "You heard my girl. You need to get your stank ass up," he said. The girl gasped, but Tripp just shrugged. She didn't move fast enough. Cyn pulled her out of Tripp's lap by her hair and clocked her upside the head and in her mouth before Devyn and Austin broke them up. Tripp was laughing.

"Yo, let her go. Chill, Cyn."

She grabbed his cup, tossed the contents in his face, and whirled around, ready to march off. He picked her up and threw her over his shoulder so fast that my jaw dropped. Cyn was screaming bloody murder. Tripp smacked her ass.

"Tell my brothers I'm gone," he said in our direction before walking off.

We all stared for a moment. "Are they always like that?" Chantal asked.

"Pretty much," Tay and I answered her simultaneously.

Devyn shook his head. "I'm jealous!"

"Why?" I asked.

He looked at me like I was crazy. "Girl, they finna fuck the hell out of each other."

I blushed. "Devyn!"

He winked at me. Shaking my head, I turned to walk into the building.

And saw Katerah chatting up a smiling Tremell.

"Whew, these niggas trying it tonight," Devyn muttered.

Ok, so yeah, I wanted to stab him. Repeatedly. With something rusty. And I wanted to smash that bitch's head into a wall for the way she looked over and smirked at me.

But I remembered that I'd suggested this.

116

"Oh, hell, no. He not finna be out here with this trick and you pregnant and shit," Tay said, I grabbed her arm.

"It's cool, Tay. For real," I added as she gave me the side eye. If he wanted that scandalous thot, he could have at it. I shot them a smile and walked right back in the building.

TREMELL

Wait, I know what y'all thinking. Yeah, I'm crazy, but not *that* crazy. Y'all saw what jealousy just made Cyn do, right? And I wanted to let Shamar know that she didn't want that, "seeing other people" shit. I mean, I was tryna do her a favor. Wasn't nobody stupid enough to step to *my* girl who was pregnant with *my* baby, unless that nigga had a death wish. On the other hand, I could run through half the women in Houston. That shit wouldn't be fair. Plus, I was mad. I know Cyn and Devyn had her all dolled up in that yellow. I wanted her sunshine reserved for *me*.

And, I ain't gone lie. Something about Katerah got to me. I don't know if it was our history or what, but I still hadn't cut her off completely. I let her apologize for that car wash stunt, so she felt free to approach when she saw me. I knew I was playing with fire—I'd already been burned, hell. But I guess my stupid ass had moth tendencies.

My Mouse was tryna play hard though. She walked into the center with her little crew like she gave no fucks about me, Katerah, or anything else.

"Damn, it's like that? If she don't mind, I don't," Katerah said, lowering her hand to rub across my crotch. I moved her hand.

"Chill, girl."

She laughed as I started walking into the building. "Tre, you know you'll be back."

I flipped her off. She laughed harder.

"Tre!" This time, it was a dude's voice. I turned to see Dmitri Giuseppe. I dapped him up.

"What brings you to a hood block party?" I said, messing with him, as we entered the center.

"Stopping through with my little bro, Anton. He knows Tavion. His sister was Anton's biology lab partner and they're good friends. I think he got a crush on her. I guess it'd be your girl's sister, too, huh?" he asked, grabbing an hors d'oeuvres plate.

He didn't even notice my steps had picked up. I was tryna practice some of them damn breathing exercises one of them doctors tried to teach me, but that shit never worked.

"Tavi ain't got but one sister."

Dmitri almost choked on the deviled egg he'd just put in his mouth.

"Aww, damn, Tre. You know I can't let you kill my little brother," he said, matching my pace.

I spotted them, then. She had her hands wrapped around a red Solo cup, while she smiled up at a tall blond dude. I'd seen the way girls flipped over Dmitri. I hoped his little brother was the ugly duckling of the family. By the time I made it to stand next to them, Mir and Tyrese were there. I knew they read my body language.

"Anton, these are three of the Kinsey brothers, Tre, Tamir, and Ty," Dmitri introduced.

"My father and brother speak highly of you," Anton said, shaking my brothers' hands. He extended his hand toward me. "Tre, you're legendary. I've heard a lot about you." I just looked at his hand until he dropped it. I was low-key mad that this nigga looked like a Dmitri-clone.

"Maybe you've heard that your friend here is his girl," said Dmitri.

"Oh, I'm not his girl," Shamar said, smiling at all of us. "If y'all will excuse us, Anton and I were in the middle of a conversation." She linked her arm through his and got ready to walk away. Dmitri, Ty, and Mir looked at me, like they were expecting something. Truth is, I *was* about to show my ass, but them niggas looking at me let me know something.

I was getting too predictable. I struggled against the blackness trying to swallow me.

"Anton." He heard me easily because the room had gotten quiet.

He turned to look at me. Youngin' had respect in his eyes, but no fear. "Hope you ain't got plans for my baby mama."

Them Italian and Russian mafia genes were suddenly on full display. "I mean, I have had my eyes on her a while. Knowing that she's single…" He shrugged and left the rest to my imagination, I guess. I laughed then.

"Nigga, I will-"

"What?" he challenged before I could finish. "Remember, my pedigree looks like yours."

"You think I give a fuck?"

Dmitri spoke up. "Y'all need to chill. We're allies in this shit. We're not about to fuck it up over some damned girl. No offense, Tre. Anton, step down."

Anton glared at his brother. "She said-"

"Step. The. Fuck. Down." In that moment, I saw why Dmitri was going to be the next head of their crime family. Anton mugged him, but he untangled his arm from Shamar's. "Let's go," Dmitri said.

Anton looked down at Shamar. He touched her face and told

120

her, "I'll be in touch." She nodded. It took everything in me not to go twist that nigga's neck until it popped. I clenched and unclenched my hands. Once the Giuseppes had cleared the building, I walked toward Shamar. "Turn the music back up!" I ordered. The DJ did so instantly. I leaned down to whisper in her ear. "I told you that you didn't wanna play this game. Because this is how it works: I do what I want. You do what I tell you." Over her shoulder, I beckoned for Katerah. She walked up and stood next to me and I grabbed her hand.

"Go home, Little Mouse," I said, pulling Katerah towards the dance floor.

I heard her tell Shamar, "Don't wait up."

Shamar

I rode home with Devyn in total silence and refused to let him come in. He and Tamar texted me until I turned off my phone and sat in the darkness. I thought I was too humiliated to cry. That is, until Ced knocked on my door and wordlessly handed me a pint of salted caramel gelato.

I broke down in his arms.

We were barely in the car before I let loose, "I can't believe your ass, nigga! First, you let that damned trollop-"

"Is that even a word anymore?" He asked.

I rolled my eyes. "TROLLOP bounce her ass up and down in your lap like she was dry fucking you. Then you gone try to check me? Like I gotta make public declarations about your ass."

I crossed my arms over my chest and rolled my eyes again so hard it hurt. He shrugged.

"It worked."

"And how dare you carry me off like that? First of all, I ain't no goddamned sack of rice. Second of all, I was having fun with my crew."

Tripp turned part of the way to look at me. "Cyn Claire, do you ever shut up? Are you ever happy? Inquiring minds wanna know!"

That was it. I started punching him in his arm and side. "If you don't like my attitude, why you tryna be my man, nigga?"

"Chill with all that fighting. I know you see me tryna drive!"

"I don't give a fuck! You ain't finna just do me any kind of way! Talking to me crazy! Who I look like? You better go get some shy bitch." I popped him after each sentence.

He tried to grab my hand and keep one hand on the wheel, but I evaded him. "Cyn, stop!"

"Or what? Huh, Tristan?" I punched his arm.

"If you put your hands on me one more time, we gone have trouble."

I ignored him. Deep down, I had to admit that Tripp was so laid back compared to my always-ready-to-pop-off ass that he let me get away with murder. I punched him again. He looked at me out the corner of his eye and smiled. I swear it was evil.

"Just remember that I told your hard-headed, mean ass."

Ok, maybe I overstepped a little. My ass sat back in my seat as he suddenly sped up and took us north on 59.

"Where we going? I wanna go home!" I whined.

"Shut the fuck up, Ma. I'm not giving a damn about what you want right now," he growled. He grilled me and between that and his tone, I was shocked into silence. We rode for 30 or 45 minutes, til we were in one of the little towns north of Houston. Tripp pulled off the highway, down a little dirt road.

He turned around and looked at me and smiled his little scary smile again. "You know what we do up here?" he asked.

I swallowed and shook my head.

"Bury people." His grin was horrible.

"Stop playing!" I was whining like I was Cynaa's age.

Tripp raised one eyebrow. "What makes you think I'm playing?"

"Tripp-"

"Uh-uh. Don't call my name now, Ms. Boosie Bad Ass." He stopped and got out. It was dark as hell. I tried to lock my door but he had the key fob. He opened my door and dragged me out. I knew Tripp wouldn't really do anything to me, but I was still scared. He swung me up in his arms and sat me on the hood of his car.

"The engine is hot!"

"Shut up, Cyn Claire!" He mugged me and his voice was

hard. I really was a little afraid, but, shit, it turned me on when he handled me rough. I love my sweet, mellow Tripp, but every once in a while, I liked for him to get my mind right. I know I'm a lot to deal with. "Now what's all that shit you were talking?"

"Umm... tonight?" I asked, like I was clueless.

"Tonight and the past couple of months. Running your damned mouth. Having an attitude. Tryna give yo weak ass baby daddy my pussy. You finna make up for all of that."

He pulled my legs open and stood between them. Shit the fact that I was scared didn't stop me from getting wet instantly. Tripp reached under my dress and ripped off my panties.

"Tristan!"

"Shut up, Cyn, I'ma do the talking for once," he said, dragging me down the hood until my ass was almost hanging off.

"Ok, you doing too much now. You not about to-" but I couldn't even finish my sentence as that nigga plunged into me. I didn't even know he had taken that damned anaconda out.

"Tripp!" That shit felt sooooo good. I had missed this so much. The fact that he was manhandling me made my pussy gush even more. He had my knees pressed damn near to my ears and was fucking me so hard it damned near hurt, but it hurt so good. He bit at my nipples through my dress. I moaned. "Tristan..."

"Shut up! It's 'Daddy' when I'm in this pussy." That shit made me cream around him instantly.

He smirked down at me as he felt me cum. "Look at you. You a god damned minute woman. I know you missed this dick." He pulled out all of a sudden and I damn near cried.

"Noooo..."

"Take all them damned clothes off." I quickly obeyed him, stripping out of my dress. He watched me while palming his dick. Before he could set me back on the car I dropped to my knees and took him into my mouth. I tasted our combined flavors and almost came again.

"That's it, baby. Suck this dick." He grabbed my head and I swear he fucked my throat. My head game is fiyah though. Wasn't no gagging on my part. I pulled off just long enough to spit on it, getting him extra wet so I could work on him with my hand and mouth. I looked up at him beneath my eyelashes. I knew that shit turned him on. "Goddamn, girl." He pulled me up, but I was hesitant to release him.

"Come on," he said.

"But you taste so good," I pouted as I stood up. He kissed me quickly then turned me around. He had me stand on one leg and then bend the other and put it on the hood. And then, he was drilling me again, his fingers playing with my nipples and my clit. Tripp was fucking me so intensely that all I could do was hold on for the ride. That shit was delicious.

My body started to shake again and I screamed out as my pussy flooded and tightened around him. I saw stars, moons, planets, angels, what the fuck ever was in the sky.

"Tell Daddy you sorry for all that nonsense you been talking," my love demanded.

"I'm sorry, Daddy," I said, breathless and holding on to the hood for dear life.

"You gone stop bossing up so much?"

"Mm-hmm. Whatever you want, baby"

He popped my ass. "Stop lying." He started grinding into me, pulling me by hair to bring me closer to him.

"Who do you belong to, Cyn?"

"This pussy is yours, Daddy," I sobbed.

"Fuck that, Cyn Claire." He stroked into me harder, angling

and hitting my walls in just the right spot. I was so wet that the sounds of him fucking me echoed in the night. I almost collapsed. "Who do your heart and mind belong to Cyn?"

Unbelievably, I was about to come again, "You, Tristan," I admitted truthfully as my pussy squeezed him for dear life. "Always you. Only you!"

"Yeah," he said. "Yeah." He came inside me as my body continued to milk him for all he was worth.

Finally, we collapsed onto the hood of the car. Had he not been lying on top of me, I probably would've slid off.

"I love you, Cyn Claire Murray," he whispered, kissing my neck repeatedly.

"I love you back, Tristan Neil Kinsey," I murmured, loving the feel of his solid, warm body against my back and his lips touching me.

He pulled back a little and smacked me on my ass. "But you better stop fucking with me."

"Yes, Daddy." I said obediently.

He stood me up and helped me re-dress, then opened my car door. When he got in, I vaguely heard him sing, "I put that ass in a coma, huh?"

It took all my energy to flip him off. I was sleep before we made it back to the highway.

In the privacy of my suite, I slow-twerked happily to Kevin Gates's "2 Phones." I was especially singing, "One for the PLUG and one for the LOAD!" My dad and brothers were so overprotective that they wanted to keep me out of the game. But after much insistence on my part, they were including me more. Today, Mir and I were going to meet with the plug. He wanted details about the hit on our crib. We had to convince him that all was okay—and it really was—or we might lose the contact.

I was determined to be taken seriously. My hair was in braids and I pulled them into a low bun. I wore a simple, cap-sleeved black sheath dress by Akris Punto and Alexander Birman nude heels that tied around the ankle and had one strap across my toes. My makeup was barely there and my full lips were done in my favorite nudes—a mix of Half-n-Half by MAC and Lolita by Kat Von D. I gave myself one last approving look before my twin knocked on the door.

"You ready?" he asked.

"How do I look?"

Tamir rolled his eyes. "Such a girl."

Appearances were important, especially since we'd been robbed. Couldn't let the supplier think we were struggling. So, we took Daddy's Phantom and a driver. We rode to the Memorial area, to a lavish mansion that made our estate look average. I knew this wasn't our contact's home, just a preapproved, safe middle ground. Tamir looked at me as the driver waited to be buzzed through the gates. I knew my twin could feel my nervousness. "Show time. You got this," he said, squeezing my hand. And, just like that, I was calm. We'd always had that bond.

We pulled up on the circular driveway and waited as our doors were opened. A butler met us at the door and showed us into an elegant sitting room done in black and white. Fresh flowers and a beautiful, abstract painting were the only splashes of color. Before we could take our seats, the most beautiful man I'd ever laid eyes on appeared. He had curly, shoulder length jet black hair. He was a couple of shades lighter than us and I read him as black and Latino. High cheekbones and a strong jaw made his face sinfully masculine, but his full lips and dark, piercing eyes made him irresistible. And his body... *Lawd Hammercy!* He wore a white v-neck shirt and some faded jeans. He was built like Ty and Tre, all thick muscles beneath gorgeous, sun-kissed skin. The only flaws on this god of a man were the scars that covered parts of his throat. He was obviously part of a security team as he let us know that he was here to "check us." His voice sounded raspy and rough, like something was wrong with his voice box. I wondered about the scars on his neck. He patted Tamir down first, from shoulders to ankles with quick skilled movements.

And then it was my turn. His firm fingers stroked against my shoulders and I sucked in my breath. He looked at me with those bottomless eyes before saying, "Arms out." I did as he requested. His fingers skimmed down my sides to the top of my hips before his hands circled to my back and rubbed down it. Nature forced me to exhale, but I couldn't move. He continued his search of my hips and thighs.

"I have to check that there is nothing strapped to your inner thighs," he grated out.

"Hey, nigga-" Tamir began.

I shook my head, looked into those dark eyes again. "It's ok, Mir," I said. The man moved quickly, his cool fingertips brushing the inside of my thighs. Sheer willpower kept me standing, because the heat that burned my skin from his touch was overpowering. This time, when those eyes met mine, I swear I saw the ghost of a smile around his lips. But then it was gone and he was standing, giving the butler a single nod. "Feel free to sit," he said.

My brother and I settled on the love seat as he eased into a chair. A moment later, a distinguished looking man with a headful of gray hair and a slight limp entered the room. He was followed by a younger version of himself. "Thank you, *Angel*," he said with a heavy Spanish accent as he settled on the couch across from us. "I am sure our guests understand why such precautions are necessary." Tamir nodded and I gave him a tight smile.

"I see that Mr. Kinsey has chosen to send one of the more beautiful members of the family. You are Tamar, no?"

"I am," I said. I wasn't surprised he knew my name—my family would have already had to vouch for me for me to be here.

"As lovely as your charming *màmà*."

"Thank you," I gave him the same little smile.

"I am Carlos and this is Pablo. And now, for the reason for your visit. I understand that someone robbed us of our blessings?" His face and voice changed almost instantly, becoming brisk and all about business.

But this is what I had prepped for. I was truthful about the extent of the hit, but confident about our ability to recoup. I hinted at our longstanding relationship and our rate of return to him. To use a common saying, this was a minor setback before a major comeback. Carlos waved his hand in the middle of one my sentences. I stopped and waited. I should care most about what he thought, but my eyes couldn't help darting to Angel. I thought I saw that glimmer of a smile again. I relaxed a little.

"You are as persuasive as you are beautiful, *querida,*" Carlos finally spoke. He stood up. "Pablo will be in touch. *Angel*, will you show them out?"

I looked at Tamir. He grinned and blew me a kiss. Relief washed through me.

"You ready?" Angel said.

I nodded and stood. He followed us to the door and I was hyper-conscious of him behind me. Suddenly, he bumped into me. Electricity sizzled between us and I was frozen. He didn't move, making it hard for me to get myself together. Finally, he stepped back and I breathed a sigh of relief.

"*Lo siento,*" I said, apologizing as if I'd run into him.

Tamir turned to look at us suspiciously and I dropped my eyes. *Ángel* didn't say anything until we reached the door. He leaned down and whispered in my ear.

"*Estás excusado, mi corazón.*"

(*You're excused, my heart.*)

I damned near ran out the door. Only when I was in the safety of the car did I dare to look at him again.

He was watching me. Those eyes penetrated my very soul.

Shamar

I pulled open the door and glared at Cyn and Devyn.

"Bitch, Tripp is babysitting and we came to get your ass out this house," Dev announced, pushing past me.

Ok, so I *had* been in my pajamas for three days. But it's not what y'all think. My humiliation was long gone. I was mad as hell now and I couldn't think of a master plan. Tremell was gon pay for what he did to me. It didn't help that Anton had been sending me flowers and random texts every day.

Cyn gave me a quick hug before strolling over to plop down beside Dev on the couch.

"So them niggas punked both y'all that night-"

"Damn. Thanks, Devyn," Cyn said dryly.

"But that shit is over with. We finna beat Tre at his own game."

I flopped down on my recliner. "Just tell me how."

Devyn gave me a look that made me feel slower than a snail. "This white boy done bought you a damned garden and you don't know what to do? You finna go out with him!"

I sighed. "For what? Tre to cause a big, messy scene?"

"That boy a Giuseppe. Let him handle his own. We just worried about making you irresistible. Text him and tell him you want to go out soon. Like, tomorrow soon."

I rolled my eyes. "Anyway. Cyn, how's it going with Tripp?"

She smiled a little. "Girl! After the night of the party, I'm just now able to walk and sit down correctly. But I put that nigga in a coma, too."

Devyn gave me an "I told you so," look. All I said was, "Eww."

"But, y'all. I know I'm wrong. Tripp's lifestyle... It'd be different if it was just me taking a risk."

"Bestie, what's Aaron's responsibility?" I asked her. She frowned.

"What do you mean?"

"She means he's a Prince and he neglected to tell you that. You gotta think about what you may have done differently to protect Naa if you knew that. I bet when you heard Tripp was going out, you woulda been on alert. And I bet Tripp woulda made sure his lady bug was out of harm's way," Devyn explained. "That man loves y'all, Cyn. This ain't all on him."

I nodded my agreement.

"I'm trying, y'all," was all she said.

"Now, you," Devyn said. "Come on in here and find something for your date tomorrow. And then we going to the movies or something."

"Dev-" But he had already disappeared into my room.

"Why you fighting him?" Cyn asked.

"I'on even know."

Tamir

"**Y**ou ain't have to do Shay like that," I told Tre as I tucked another bill into the thong of the girl currently giving me a lap dance.

Tre looked at me, looked at the dancer, and said, "I'on think you should be giving relationship advice."

"You gon fuck around and lose her. Then yo ass gon wanna kill everybody in H-town," Tripp grilled Tre as he spoke.

"I'm not gon lose her. Shorty ain't going nowhere. But she gotta learn she can't disrespect me. I let her make it at the club. I let Devyn live because of her. And then she think she finna deny me and talk to some nigga in my face? Nah. I got a reputation to uphold. People ain't finna be crossing me because they think I'm weak," Tre said, taking his drink from the server and tipping her $100.

"Shiiiiiit, with Cyn and Devyn in her ear, you finna have hell," Tripp warned.

"Tay talking shit, too," I added. "They bout to have that girl *all* hyped up."

Tre frowned. "Shamar better sit the fuck down and grow my seed."

"Man, fuck these girls," Ty muttered as he took a swallow of his Hennessy.

"I didn't say all that, nigga," Tre shot back.

Me and my brothers were supposed to be having a meeting about our next step in the Prince situation. The only things that had been decided was that we were gon take one of his family members to try to flush him out and that we were about to start setting traps to catch our own snake. After that, everybody started talking about other shit. I knew we had to get shit right in our personal lives. Distraction could cause death in our business.

"Who pissed in your Cheerios?" I asked Ty. He just shook his head and took another long swallow.

"I'm just saying. They want you to play their games and be at their beck and call. Who got time for that? I'm tired of games and shit."

All of us looked at Ty in shock. "*You* tired of games?" Tripp asked. "It's that damned doctor ain't it?" He turned to me and Tre, laughing. "Bout damned time, way you was bluesing us! A little ol' bougie girl got this nigga nose wide open."

"That part ain't funny," Tre's sensitive ass said.

"Fuck you, Tripp. She ain't got my nose open. She wanna play a game I refuse to play." He shrugged. "Too bad for her. Too much pussy in the world for that and definitely too much being thrown my way. I'on blame Tre for fucking Katerah."

Tre choked on his Rey Sol Anejo before putting his glass down. "I ain't fuck that girl. Not taking the risk of exposing my girl and my baby to nothing."

Ty looked at him in disbelief. "You stupid as hell, then."

"Sho' is." Tripp's comment surprised me—I knew he was a fan of Shay—until he followed it up with, "You shoulda got something to tide you over cuz I bet Shay ain't gone even let you look at it! I wouldn't."

"Nigga, I wouldn't want to see yours."

Another dancer came along and asked if I wanted a lap dance. I declined, threw some bills on the table, and stood up. "I gotta go. DuBois went grocery shopping yesterday, so I know she throwing down in that kitchen tonight," I said.

Ty shook his head. "Ol' homebody ass. You were my last hope."

"Shiiiiit, nigga, way you acting, when that doctor put it on you, all your hope gone be gone," I snapped back. "When we gon meet her anyway?"

Some look passed over his face before he said, "Never," and downed the rest of his drink.

I left my big brothers to work that out. Just as I suspected, when I got home, DuBois was in the kitchen prepping. I saw herbs, lemons, olives, tomatoes, and chicken among other things. Baby was a damned gourmet chef. She had been cooking since she was 11 because her parents, both doctors, worked long hours and she and her sister and brother had to fend for themselves sometimes.

"Hey," I greeted her. "What you making?"

"Hey. It's based on a dish called Chicken Provencal, but I change it a little." She looked beautiful as ever in her tank top and short shorts. She had her hair pulled up into a ponytail and her face was bare of makeup. I'on know why she wore it anyway. Her skin was the most perfect I'd ever seen, deep brown and glowing without any blemishes. Her lashes were longer than some of the fake ones chicks sported and her lips looked full and juicy without lipstick.

"Little Mama sleep?" I asked.

"Mm-hmm."

I was about to walk out the kitchen when I stopped and turned to her. "Ay, you need some help?"

She looked at me in surprise. "You cook now?"

I shrugged. "You right," I said and walked toward the doorway.

"Tamir?" I loved the way she said my name. Everyone else called me "Tuh-mir," but with her little bit of accent, she said "Tah-mir."

"Huh?"

"You can help."

I washed up quickly. Shorty had me slicing lemons and olives and scraping an herb she called rosemary off the stem. She even had me trying to dice a bell pepper and onion. DuBois laughed when my eyes teared up. "Next time hold a piece of bread or a match in your mouth," she advised.

"What?"

"I don't know why, but it works."

The kitchen smelled good as she browned the chicken. As the room heated up, little pieces of her hair started to curl around her face and she looked adorable. I crossed my arms over my chest and leaned against the counter as she put the dish together and got ready to stick it in the oven. My healthy, happy baby was upstairs sleep and her beautiful mama was in my kitchen in my spotless, well-decorated house. I know I'm young, but a nigga felt lucky as hell.

"Mir, why you looking at me like that?" she asked, self-conscious. She brushed her hair back and checked her clothes for spots.

"Nothing's wrong, DuBois. You just look good doing that," I told her.

She smiled and shook her head. "You so silly."

"Come here," I told her. She looked nervous but she walked over to stand in front of me. I brought my hands up to cup her face. "I appreciate all you doing around here. I appreciate that my baby got an excellent mama. And most of all… I appreciate how that ass sitting up in them shorts."

She swung at me, but she was laughing. And just like that, I leaned in and kissed her. She tasted as sweet as always and her lips… *Damn.* Her hands went around my wrists, but she just held on and kissed me back. I turned us around and picked her up to set on the counter. Her arms linked around my neck and my hands went to her thighs. I spread them to make room for myself, then slid my hands under her little shirt to stroke her back. She arched into me and moaned against my mouth—her back was sensitive. I let my fingers trail down her spine to the top of her plump ass. Noah had put weight on her in all the right places. She surprised me by reaching for my shirt. I stripped out of that bitch with a quickness and watched as she traced the tattoo of her face.

"I love this," she murmured.

"Conceited ass."

She pushed me a little and hopped down. I thought I had pissed her off until her arms went around my waist and she leaned forward to kiss my chest. She licked across my nipple before sucking it a little bit. Shit, I ain't gone lie. That felt good. My soldier immediately went on brick.

"What you tryna do, ma?" I asked her. She looked up at me with her eyes half closed. Her hands crept down to rub against my dick. "Oh, you want that?"

"Mm-hmm," she said, while nodding.

I picked her up and walked into the living room where I laid her on the couch before I got on top of her. I kissed her again, biting gently on her lips.

"Tamir… I missed you," she said, breathless as she pressed her lips against my throat.

"Missed you, too, shorty," I told her, settling between her legs. I captured her mouth again and my hands went to her shorts, easing them down her legs. The little white lacy panties she had on had me wanting to rip them away.

"Damn, DuBois!"

She thrust her pelvis upward, rubbing that pussy against me.

"Now, Mir. I don't wanna wait," her tone was pleading. A beautiful ass woman begging for the dick? That shit was the biggest turn on ever. I was out of my pants and boxer briefs in two seconds, slinging my wallet and my phone to the floor, and I could feel how wet her pussy was through her panties. She pushed me back far enough to flip over on her stomach, her favorite position. Right across her ass were the words, "Try me." *You ain't gotta tell me twice!* I pulled them panties to the side—a nigga didn't want to wait to take them down. I was ready—had myself at her tight, wet opening.

And my phone chimed its text message sound. We both looked down at the floor. I couldn't believe this shit as the name "Daria" popped up on the screen. DuBois froze instantly.

"Ugh! Get off me with your lying ass!" she screamed. I was so shocked that this bitch was texting me after all this time that I let DuBois up. She grabbed her shorts and stomped into the kitchen.

I opened the message.

DARIA:

> So you entertaining that bitch again but you can't make time for your son?

I typed faster than I ever had in life.

139

ME:

Bitch, I'm gon find yo trifling ass
tomorrow and give you to Tre.

I wasn't surprised when she didn't respond. But this trick was
gon pay.

The next day, I got Ty to ride with me to the hood to check
Daria. I wanted to make sure I didn't end up in jail. We took my
Audi and Ty rolled up a blunt full of kush, but I swear that nigga
slipped some moon rocks in on me. I could only take a couple of
puffs because it felt like I was about to be high as FUCK! Daria
has medium brown skin, but that bitch turned damn near white
when she opened the door and saw me and my brother standing
there. She tried to close it real fast, but I held it open. Me and Ty
walked in and seated ourselves on her fake leather furniture.
Daria screamed at us to get out of her house.

"I can't stand you, Mir. Stay away from me!"

"That ain't what your bitch ass said in that text message.
Why you keep tryna wreck my happy home, you stupid ho? I just
came to tell you to lose my number. In fact, lose yo memory
when it comes to me."

She swung at me but I easily moved out the way. "Was I a ho
when you were fucking me?"

Ty looked at her like she was crazy. "Yeah. That's why he
fucked you. Cause you were a ho."

"Shut up, Tyrese," she yelled, picking up a coaster and
throwing it at him. Ty caught it and threw it back, smacking her
in the forehead. Daria's mouth dropped open, like she couldn't
believe it. Ty shrugged.

"You know I played varsity baseball, ma," he said. I don't

know if it was the weed or what, but that shit was super funny to me. I laughed until I cried, rolling all over her couch, while she screamed at me. But I cut that shit off abruptly when I heard a door open and someone start walking down the stairs. Ty and I both reached for our bangers. "It's just my boyfriend," she hissed. I still kept my hand on my piece, tucked in the back of my waistband, though. A white man with no shirt and a big ass belly came into view. He was holding an extremely light-skinned baby in his arms.

"Daria, what in the world is going on? You and your friends woke up Robert, Jr.," he looked annoyed and she looked embarrassed.

Ty mugged her. "Girl, this light bright baby is the one you tryna lay on my brother after you done named him after some other dude? I swear you take trifling to a new level."

She had the decency to look down.

"Yo, Robert, Sr.?" He looked at me uncertainly. "Tell your girl if she texts or calls me again talking about Robert, Jr. is mine, my sister Tay and her girls coming to beat that ass. Make sure she blocks my number. Matter of fact, I'm getting that bitch changed."

Ty and I left then. Soon as we walked out the door, I heard arguing. Looked like Robert, Jr. was gone be woke for a while.

"I'ma stop at Target," I told Ty. He groaned. Target was my shit, man. I walked around in there just picking up stuff and wasting money. It relaxed my mind. I was already feeling mellow by the time we pulled into the parking lot.

"I ain't staying in here for no three hours with you," Ty threatened. I ignored him and pulled out a cart. Thirty minutes into our trip, he was cussing me out and I was tryna pick out a sketchpad for DuBois.

"You don't even know what kind of art supplies she likes! I bet the shit don't come from no Target!"

"Shut up, nigga, it's the thought that counts!"

"Excuse me!" A voice said from behind us. Ty and I both turned with mugs on our faces. It didn't help that Ty had on his gold and diamond grill—swear that nigga keeps Johnny Dang rich—and was sneering. Some square ass dude was standing there needing to get by. I was about to get fly with the nigga cause I didn't like his tone, then I noticed the lady he had his arm around. My mug disappeared.

"Hey, Dr. Rose! Good to see you," I said, leaning forward to give her a hug. She smiled at me as we broke apart.

"You're looking good, Tamir."

"Thanks to you." I looked over at Ty. He was still looking mean. "Bro, this my surgeon, Dr. Rose. Dr. Rose, this is my brother."

She blushed a little. "I remember seeing him. Tyrese, right?" He just looked at her for a minute before nodding. "Tamir, Tyrese, this is my friend and colleague, Brennan." Brennan extended his hand and I shook it. Ty barely slapped his palm. This nigga was acting crazy. I didn't realize coming to Target would aggravate him so much.

"I guess we gon go on and head out. Dr. Rose, I'll see you soon," I said, ready to get my ignorant ass brother out the store.

Ty spoke up then. "Dr. Rose, you really look different with clothes on." Her face went completely red and her friend's mouth dropped open. "Regular clothes, I mean. Used to you in that white jacket," he added, smiling for the first time.

"Of-of course. Thanks. Bye." Her words were all rushed together, and she was clearly embarrassed as she damned near ran off.

"Why you do that, nigga? She a good lady!" I asked Ty.

He shrugged. "Fuck that broad."

I shook my head and grilled him. Then, some shit clicked. "Yo! You sneaky ass nigga. *My doctor*? You tryna fuck *my doctor*?" I laughed at his ass then, because his face let me know it was true. "Good for yo ass that she turned you down. She got class-"

"Guess that's why she let me eat that pussy on her office desk," he shot back. I got serious then.

"She cool people, Ty. You play with these hoes too much. Leave her alone. Let her have niggas like Brennan."

"Fuck you, man. You sound like her. She ain't too good for me! I'll meet your lame ass outside!"

This shit-talking nigga done got sensitive on us? What the fuck?

I paid for my stuff and walked out. Ty didn't talk to me all the way home and when he got out, he slammed my door. I couldn't help it. I cracked up at that nigga again. I let down the window and yelled at him, "Get out yo chest, ol' pussy ass nigga!" He didn't even turn around. I laughed most of the ride home. DuBois's car was there, so I knew she was in the house. She wasn't in the kitchen or living room. I sat down on the couch and picked up her sketchbook. The first few pages were drawings of Noah. Every line and shade reflected her love for our little girl. I traced some of the images with my fingers. Shorty was so talented. Her eye for anything artistic was unbeatable.

Some of the sketches showed what she had planned for our house. The way she had it looking, we were gone be up in some of them magazines that showcase houses. I smiled at that thought —I bought this place empty and cold, but having DuBois and

143

Noah here plus DuBois's skills were turning it into a home. I kept flipping.

And I found the sketches of me. No lie, this girl made me look… I don't know. But I know if that's how she saw me, then she was still in love with me. They were all carefully done, some just of me, some of me holding Noah, and some of the three of us as a family. I loved the ones with our baby, but my favorite was one of me and DuBois. I was sitting on the couch in just a pair of jeans. My dreads were on top of my head and she was sitting in my lap with just a t-shirt on. Her face was buried in my neck and my hands were holding her close as I looked down at her. The detail was so good that she'd even drawn some of my tattoos. Just the thought of her straddling me like that, had my shit hard. Holding on to the book, I ran up the stairs.

I knocked on her bedroom door but got no answer. I was determined to talk to her though, so I cracked it. When I heard the sounds from the shower, I started grinning. She could lie all she wanted, but this little stubborn Somali-French girl loved me. I started stripping at her door. By the time I made it to the bathroom, I was naked. She gasped when I pulled back the shower curtain and stepped in.

"What do you think you're doing, Tamir? Get out! Go bathe with your other baby mama!"

I pulled her against me, even as she fought me. "I done told you. I don't have another baby mama and ain't trying to get one." Then, I kissed her. She struggled at first. But I slipped my hand between us and found her clit. Her body jerked and she moaned, even as she punched me in the shoulder.

"Tah-mir! Stoppppp," she begged, even as her hips moved against my hand.

"You stop. I saw your sketches. Tell me you don't love me, DuBois."

She pouted. "I-" but she couldn't finish that lie. I smiled triumphantly.

"Where's the baby?" I whispered.

"With Tay."

"Good. I don't want you to wake her up when you scream." I kneeled down in front of her, not caring that the water was beating down on my shoulders and my dreadhead. "Do me a favor, DuBois."

She shook her head. "We can't. I'm-I'm mad at youuuuu." The last word dissolved into a moan as I ran my finger across her clit.

"Hold that bar above your head. Don't let it go, no matter what."

"Tamir…"

I looked up at her. "Do it!"

Slowly, she raised her hands and grabbed the bar. I rewarded her with a smile then stuck my face in her center. DuBois talked to me in soft, broken French as I worked her over with my tongue. She was so sweet, like pineapples and the brown sugar body wash she used. As I sucked on her pearl, I knew I was driving her out of her mind because she told me she loved me over and over again. My tongue slid between her lips and I pushed one, then two fingers into her tight wetness. She sobbed my name. Lifting her legs, I placed one over each shoulder. She was grinding her hips against my face. Her hands came down to stroke my braided dreads. I popped her on her bubble shaped ass.

"What I tell you, DuBois?" I scolded her. Her hands returned to the bar. I swirled my tongue inside of her.

"Tamir, baby, I'm going to cuuuuummmmm," she screamed, bucking against my face.

I moved my tongue more quickly against her bud, then sucked it into my mouth as I stuck a finger in her tight little ass. I had to hold her up as she busted all over my face, her sweet essence drenching my mouth and chin. Standing up, I kissed her again, letting her taste herself. My dick was rock hard and I pulled her legs around my hips. I dragged the tip of my shaft between the lips of her sex.

"Can I have it, beautiful, brown baby?" I whispered in her ear.

Her glazed eyes tangled with mine. "Tamir... *please.*"

"Please what? Tell me I can have it," I demanded, pushing the tip into her and holding still. Shit was killing me, but I didn't want her to express regrets later. She looked at me and nodded.

"Say it," I ordered, pushing in a little farther.

"You can have it, Tah-mir," she said breathlessly.

"Have what?" I asked.

Her eyes met mine again. "My pussy. *Your* pussy. Me. Baby, please-"

I pushed inside of her with one big stroke and she cried her pleasure. She was as tight and wet as ever and I had a feeling this wouldn't be long. I started talking to her as I thrust into her.

"You love me?"

She nodded as she slid up and down my dick.

"You missed this dick?"

"Mm-hmm," she moaned.

"We gone work this out?"

"Y-yes, Tamir." She let go of the bar again to wrap her arms around my neck as she worked her hips against me.

"Nuh-uh, hard-headed girl," I said. DuBois grabbed it again as I long-stroked into her.

"Tamir, I'm cumming," she wailed. I looked down as my dick disappeared and re-appeared. Her cream was all over me. I was so turned on that I didn't give a damn about the cold shower water or anything else.

"I'm ready to change Noah's last name." She nodded as her tremors began and her walls squeezed me over and over. Just before I released into her, I put my lips against her ear. "I'm going to change yours, too."

ANGEL CRUZ

Handling security was a trade that ran in my family. My cousin, Daniel Cruz, and I designed systems together. Although Houston was his home base, I was usually in Atlanta. But Daniel didn't get into the other shit I was into. His mama came from oil money so he hadn't had to hustle as hard as I did. My security extended to protection.

And elimination. I was a contract killer, a murderer for hire, a hit man. I don't give a damn what you call me as long as you pay me. Few people were in my league—I knew a couple of people from organized crime families. And because I spent a lot of time in Houston, I knew of Tre Kinsey. That nigga had been locked down til several months ago, however, and didn't seem eager to come back into the business. So my Texas contracts were picking up. Being asked to upgrade Carlos Medrano's security team was just one example.

I thought back to the day at the Memorial mansion. The pictures Carlos had provided had not done Tamar Noelle Kinsey justice. That chick was bad from the top of her head to the soles of her designer stilettos. She was tall and had a perfect hourglass shape and her face was kissed by God. I wondered what she'd look like with her hair down, spread across my pillows, as she writhed underneath me. I didn't spend much time or thought on women, but I might have to have her.

I climbed out of my S-Class Coupe and walked into the wing joint. After a few minutes, I picked up my carry out order. The young cashier looked at me with wide, scared eyes. I smirked at her. I had that effect on people. I tipped her $200. She tried to call me back, probably to let me know I left too much money, but I ignored her. Back at my hotel, I pulled out the box of sweet habanero wings—yeah, I liked my food spicy. I also extracted the envelope that was shoved into the bottom of the bag.

My next project—this one was going to cost my contact a cool million. Sitting at the desk in the living area of the suite, I opened the envelope and grabbed the folder inside. I opened it.

And reached for my phone. It rang once before it was picked up on the other end.

"Daniel. I need you to get me a meeting."

Shamar

(One week later)

I had to admit; I was cute pregnant. Once I got past the first trimester, my skin was healthy, my hair was growing, and my little bump was the cutest thing. I admired myself in my blue and white maxi dress, whirling in front of the mirror.

Anton and I were going on our third date. With Cyn and Devyn's help, I'd sneaked out. I didn't want Tremell's drama. Plus, I didn't think for a minute I was fooling Ced. I think he just felt sorry for me. I'd already known I liked Anton from lab, but he turned out to be even funnier and more charming in a casual setting. We'd met for coffee first, then dinner at Sambuca, where he actually got me to dance a little to the live music. "Exercise is good for the baby," he coaxed. He didn't seem to be at all bothered by my pregnancy and asked me every day how I was feeling and how the baby was doing. Tonight, we were going to The Palm.

I heard a key in the door. I rolled my eyes. Shoulda known Cyn didn't trust me to dress myself. "Bitch, come in here. I look gawgeous."

To say I was surprised when Tremell appeared in my bedroom doorway would be a severe understatement. He hadn't shown his face in almost two weeks and I assumed he and Katerah were somewhere living happily ever after. He texted to check on me and the baby, but I responded through Cyn and

Tripp. I had been standing there smiling with my hand on my hip, waiting to see Cyn's pretty, brown face. My smile disappeared and I turned away from him.

"How long you gone ignore me, Shamar?"

"Hello, Tremell," I said coldly, sliding my hoops into my ears.

"You said you wanted me to date you. I'm here to take you out. Let's go."

I could see his reflection in the mirror in front of me. I looked at him incredulously. "Are you serious? You must be crazy! I haven't even seen you since you humiliated me in front of hundreds of people. I wouldn't cross the street with you! I have plans anyway."

He frowned. "Where you think you going and why you got all these damned flowers everywhere?" he asked, touching the vase on my dresser.

"None of your business." I watched as he walked up on me. He surprised me by turning me around.

"Yo, you seeing that little dude I warned you about?"

I met his eyes defiantly. "He's a grown ass man. And yes, I am." His eyes flashed at me.

"Is that why you look like this now?" He grabbed my dress. I nodded. "You think it's a fucking game, Shamar? Ain't no fucking way another man gone be around my baby like that. I'ma kill that nigga."

"And you'll start a war. Is that fair to your brothers? Y'all already caught up in other shit. Careful not to spread yourself thin, Tremell. Even *you* are human," I taunted him. I gasped as his hand went around my throat. I could tell it took everything in him not to squeeze. I didn't move, terrified, but determined he wasn't going to keep treating me like he did at the party. I breathed a sigh of relief when he dropped his hand. "Go find your fuck-buddy Katerah. Order her around. Leave me the fuck alone. If it's not about this baby, I don't wanna talk to you."

I knew by his eyes the moment he was totally gone. He just smiled at me though. As he walked out of my room, he pushed the vase off the dresser. I didn't dare go out. I heard repeated crashes and the sound of breaking glass in the living room. Shaking my head, I sat on the bed. Finally, I heard the door slam. I got my mind together—no sneaking this time. I was grown, Tremell didn't own me, and I was about to leave.

I went back to my parents' house to put some shit together. Shamar was going on a date? I was going with them. I was trying, for Dmitri's sake, not to kill his little brother. But there was only so much I was willing to put up with. It was about respect, for me and my seed. On my way back down the curved stairway, my mama saw me.

"Stop," she said. I cursed inside, but I never disrespect Mama. Ever.

"Ma'am?"

"What's going on with you, Tremell? Is this about Shay?"

I sighed. "I got business to take care of, Ma. No disrespect, but I'on wanna go into it with you."

Mama crossed her arms over her chest and waited. *Shit.*

"She carrying my baby and tryna fuc—sorry—tryna be with some other nigga."

She raised an eyebrow. "Weren't you just with some other girl? One you know means you no good?"

"I ain't mess with that girl!"

She reached out and popped my forehead. "Who you talking to, Tremell Nicholas Kinsey?! Lower your tone."

I wanted to remind her that I was grown, but all I said was, "Yes, ma'am."

"Now tell me why you can dish it out, but you can't take it?"

"Shamar and the people around her stay disrespecting me.

Then she out with some other dude, prolly got him thinking he gone play daddy. I ain't having it!" I explained.

"So what's your plan for tonight? I can tell by your eyes you ready to wreak havoc."

"Finna join her on her date. Might flip some tables and whoop some ass." I shrugged.

"And how you think she gone react? What good is it gone do?"

"I'll-"

She interrupted me. "I, I, I! That's all I hear. What about her? What about my grandbaby? You keep talking about respect, what about love, Tremell? Respect makes you show out. Do you love her?"

I paused for one minute before speaking. "Yeah. Yeah, I love that silly ass girl."

"Then what will your love make you do? You so worried about looking weak…" She grabbed my face and pulled me to her to kiss my cheek. "Baby. It's ok to be vulnerable for the ones you love when they love you just as much back. And that girl *loves* you. Your mama knows. So what if, this one time, you act out of love, Tremell?"

I shook my head. "Ma, I got a name and reputation to protect in these streets-"

"You're more worried about the streets than your home?"

I hated that she was making sense. I knew she was right, in a way. But the thought of Shamar out with someone else, laughing with him, liking him, falling in love with him…

"Do you trust me?" she asked, breaking up my thoughts.

"With my life," I said, no hesitation.

She took my hands in hers. "Then do this for me. This one time, baby, act out of love."

Inside, I was dying. But no way was I telling my mama "no." I blew out a long breath.

"Fine, Ma."

She kissed me again. "Thank you. Now take your ass back up them stairs and I bet not catch you sneaking out to kill nobody!"

My phone buzzed as I made my way back to my suite. I recognized the number of an associate who designed security systems for my parents and Shamar. I frowned, worried that one or the other had been compromised.

"Wazzam?" I answered.

"Hey, Tre. My cousin needs to meet with you and Tripp. I think you and he might be in the same line of work," Daniel Cruz said cryptically.

My mug got worse. "The fuck, Daniel? You know I-"

"His name is Angel Cruz," Daniel interrupted me. Now that made me pause. Angel Cruz might be the one nigga as throwed off and as deadly as I am. "Why would I meet with somebody I don't know for a reason I don't know?" *Why would I meet with somebody who had probably been sent to kill me?* Daniel was a security expert and this call was probably untraceable, but I didn't trust phone lines enough to say that out loud.

"He said it's about a job, but not the way you'll probably think. Tre, trust me. You need to see him."

My eyes narrowed. "Why should I trust you? The nigga is your cousin."

Daniel sighed. "Because if he wanted to do something dirty to your family, he already could have. He helped design the systems I installed for y'all. And he sat in on a business meeting with Mir and Tay."

True. Plus, I was curious and confident. I doubted the nigga could take me and Tripp. "Tell him to meet me ASAP at the basketball courts. You know which ones. Tell him I won't show my face til I see him under the light. And if this ain't right, I'm coming to visit your whole family."

"Damn, Tre," Daniel said before hanging up.

I hurriedly called Tripp and he agreed to meet me at the park. Mama didn't want to let me out—I had to put it on *her* life that I wasn't going to confront Shamar and Anton. Tripp and I waited silently near a darkened area by some bleachers. Finally, a figure stepped out of the darkness to stand under one of the lights that illuminated the court and close by areas. He held out both his hands and one of them had what looked like a folder. Tripp and I moved toward him, guns drawn. Angel's expression didn't change.

"You know what I do for a living?" he asked us.

"You know what I do?" I shot back. He smiled a little.

"Not sure how you get your info, but I always get a picture of my intended and a little bit of a description. My latest is in this envelope. I want you to take it."

I grilled the nigga. "Why the fuck would I take a job for you? I ain't working like that right now unless it's family business."

He had the nerve to laugh. I started to shoot the nigga on pure principle. "I don't want you to take the job. I want you to take the envelope. I think you'd be interested."

"Why you think that?" Tripp asked, his tone suspicious.

Angel shrugged. "Trust me. I'ma slide it across the ground to you," he said, moving to bend down. Tripp and I both cocked our guns.

"Move slow, nigga," I warned. He slid the envelope toward us. Tripp kept his gun trained on him as I took the few steps to pick it up. I watched him as I opened the envelope and pulled out its contents. Finally, I looked down at what I held.

"*Fuck*, no!"

Tripp looked over at me. "Who is it, Tre?"

I shook my head. "Man, it's Tay. These bitches put a hit out on our baby sister." I lifted my gun again as Tripp went into a rant. "How much, Angel? What, you want a counter offer? I'll blow your fucking head off now-"

"I paid the $1 million bounty on her head and made it clear that she better never be a target again," he said. Something told me the nigga was telling the truth and I always trusted my instincts.

"Why would you do that and why would you warn us? You got something against the dude who ordered the hit?"

Angel shrugged. "Nah. And I know it's Prince. I've done excellent business with him in the past. I'm telling you in case he doesn't take me seriously and tries it again. You can step up her detail."

Tripp looked at him sideways. "What else?"

"I met your sister. She's the most beautiful woman I have ever seen."

I lowered my gun. "So let me get this straight. You basically lost $2 million because you got a crush on my little sister?"

"Think again, nigga," Tripp broke in. "You ain't got a chance. She marrying some doctor or lawyer type and living a calm life."

Angel laughed again. "Your sister knows the game better than most of the niggas I ever worked with. You can tell it's in her blood." He turned to me. "Nah, it ain't no high school crush shit. She a queenpin in the making. I'ma be her king. I'm staying in Houston til y'all get this mess sorted out. I'm going to be the invisible part of her detail."

"First of all, Tay's king is Pops. She's a Daddy's girl. Second of all, we don't need your help. Thanks for the heads up," I told him.

"I'm sorry if I've given you niggas the impression that I need your permission or give a fuck what y'all think."

"Nigga, who the fuck you talking to?" Tripp aimed his gun and cocked it again.

"Chill," I told him. "This dude is delusional if he thinks we finna let our sister hook up with a hit man."

He tilted his head to one side. "I wonder if Tavion said the same thing?"

I ignored that. "Stay away from her."

Angel smiled. "Tre… you know me because you know yourself. So you know damned well how this is about to go down. Goodnight."

We watched as that nigga slipped into the shadows.

"*Fuck!*" Tripp cursed. "Alonzo Prince gotta go, man. We been doing this hide and seek shit with his ass too long. We gotta find that bitch and put him out of his misery."

"Chill. Ty nem gon be on their way to Dallas tonight to 'pick up' Prince's son. He gon pay for putting a hit on her. I told Ty to grab whoever else they could. We'll have them bitches by tomorrow."

Pretty soon, I'd be sending some nigga straight to hell.

TYRESE

(*The next day: Friday*)

She texted me. I hadn't talked to Briar since we ran into her and that nerdy ass nigga up in Target. I made sure I wasn't around when she checked on JB. Of course, the fact that she saved his life meant he was totally in her corner and was harassing me every day about getting with her. No way would I tell him she didn't want me like that. He assumed I was hoing around and losing her.

I texted her back. But I didn't respond how she wanted. She was gon' have to work for this good dick. I had another idea.

> ME:
>
> Job tonight. Can you ride out of town in case something happens?

Long pause, then:

> MY FAIRYTALE:
>
> Ride where?

> ME:
>
> The Metroplex.

Another minute before she responded.

MY FAIRYTALE:

> Yeah... Off tomorrow. But, Tyrese, I
> need more detail!

ME:

> I'll scoop you tonight. You won't be in
> danger. Bring clothes—we'll probably
> stay the night.

MY FAIRYTALE:

> Tyrese...

I didn't respond. Instead, I picked her up around six that evening. She had a little bag with her and a backpack. I put her shit in the trunk then took off.

"Will it be like last time?" she asked after a few minutes.

"Hopefully, everything goes smooth. But if not, we gotta place you can set up shop. While we working, I'ma put you in a hotel. If I need you, I'll come get you. You get paid either way, if you're worried."

She looked down. "I wasn't worried about that, Tyrese. You keep saying 'we.' Are we picking up someone?"

I shook my head. "Nah. They driving separately, nosey."

Our ride was silent for a few more minutes. Then she spoke again. "The way you acted in Target was rude. You didn't have to-"

"It wasn't rude for you to act like you didn't know me?" I shot back, mugging her little sadiddy ass. She sighed.

"I was caught off guard."

"Didn't want your nigga to know I tasted the goodies?" I smirked at her.

It was Briar's turn to grill me, only her "mad" face was

adorable. "See? That's uncalled for. And Brennan is not my nigga."

"I'on think he knows that, the way he had his hands all over you."

"You're exaggerating, Tyrese."

I looked at her out the corner of my eye. "Tell me that nigga ain't tryna get in them draws." She took in a deep breath then blew it out like she was frustrated. I knew I was right. Who could blame him, though?

"Your mouth is so vulgar!"

"I thought that was one of the things you liked about me," I said, pretending to be hurt.

"Ugh! Just turn on some music!"

I purposely turned to an old school rap and hip hop satellite station that was full of "vulgar" language. She surprised me, though. Trick Daddy and Trina's "Nann" came on and she rapped every bit of Trina's part. She got especially loud when she rapped:

Now you don't know nann hoe, uh uh
That'll ride the dick on the dime
Who love to fuck all the time
One who's pussy fatter than mine

I just looked at her in shock. For some reason, hearing her spit that X-rated shit had me needing to adjust my soldier in my pants. "That's how you coming?" I asked her.

She gave me a little half smile. "You don't know nann, Tyrese."

For the rest of the three-hour ride, we talked and rapped old school songs. I found myself enjoying the time with Briar Rose. I'm a hit it and quit it type of nigga, so I don't usually take the time to really talk to broads. They can top me off, get their backs banged out, and then I'm gone. But something was different about this one and I'd known that since the first time I saw her at the hospital. Hell, she was only the second woman I'd put my mouth on and I couldn't wait to taste her again. This little fairytale doctor was gon be mine. But it was gon be on my terms, not hers. I hadn't had a real relationship since me and my high school sweetheart broke up when we were 18. I could imagine chilling with Briar one-on-one, though. I smirked as I thought about all the hoes I was about to make miserable when I took myself off the market.

"What you smiling about?" she asked me.

"Thinking about how I'ma make you say a few vulgar words of your own when you taking this dick."

Her eyes got big. "Oh my God, Tyrese! You have no filter!"

"I got a huge dick, though. Just so you can be prepared. That pussy was tight around my fingers, so I know I'ma have to break it in." She covered her ears with her hands while I laughed.

I checked us into the Grand Hyatt DFW. With a few extra stacks, I was able to avoid showing an ID or using a credit card. Briar looked at me and shook her head, but didn't say a word. I helped her get settled in the room. She eyed the one King bed. I shrugged and she rolled her eyes.

"Yo, you should relax if you can. They got that big ass TV and the bathroom has a shower and a tub, if you want to soak. And order a bottle of something good. I know chicks be liking bubble baths and wine," I told her.

"Stereotyping self! But a bubble bath sounds good."

"I gotta go catch up with my team. You gon be good, Ma?" I

asked her. I really wanted her to be okay and I hoped I didn't have to bring no banged up niggas back to her.

"Ty, this place is nicer than my house. I'm going to take a long bath and order everything on the room service menu to be charged to you," she teased.

"Do that," I said. And because it just felt right, I walked over to her and dropped a kiss on her lips. She blushed but touched my face.

"Please be careful."

I grinned at her. "Girl, I ain't dying before I break you off and break you in."

"TYRESE!"

I left without another word. I had the location memorized and Bones had already destroyed the security system. He met me up the street to brief me. "These niggas is sad, Ty. Alonzo's son posted up in the house, talking to two chiefs about moving product too slow. We already took the guards out, so they up in there with three of the most important people in their organization unprotected and they stupid asses don't even realize."

I shook my head. They meeting up altogether like that with weak ass protection? It wasn't like it was some fancy mansion that was reinforced or a neighborhood that was patrolled. It was a trap one step up from the hood. Somebody failed The Game 101.

"Rest of our soldiers?" I asked.

"Got the house surrounded."

"You ready?" I asked.

Bones grinned.

"Always," he said. No wonder he and Tre had some kinda crazy bond. We jogged back down to the house and crept up to the front door. I nodded. Bones kicked that bitch in. Stephen

Prince and his goons jumped. I had to give it to them; they reacted quickly. The chiefs tried to grab their pieces, but me and Bones were ready. I shot one in the arm and Bones got the other in the shoulder. That gave Prince a chance. Nigga had pulled a gun from somewhere. He aimed at me and fired. I moved fast, but I still felt a stinging burn on the side of my head and blood started dripping in my eyes. Prince tried to run out the house but my men were already coming through the back. My soldier Darius clocked him twice in the head with his piece, knocking him out.

Yo, this bitch almost shot me in the head? Weak ass nigga could've bodied me! I walked over to where he was crumpled up and kicked him over onto his back. I was so mad I couldn't fucking think as I aimed between his eyes. I pulled the trigger, but Bones hit my hand and the bullet went into the wall.

"Calm down, nigga. You know we need him for leverage and for information. You can off him later!" he said. I took a couple of deep breaths.

Then, I still shot that nigga in the leg. Damned fuckboy.

"Acting like your crazy ass brother," Bones muttered.

I thanked him.

After we tied them up and stripped them of their phones and wallets, we searched the house for goodies. I smiled when Bones and Jalen came back with bricks and bags of cash. I heard Darius yell, "Hey, yo, Ty!" from upstairs. I frowned and ran up there with Jalen and Bones close behind. Darius and two other men were in the first room at the top of the stairs. They parted to allow us to enter. What I saw made me wanna go back and shoot all them cowards in the nuts.

A small woman was tied to the bed. Her hair was matted around her head and her lips were dry and cracked. Whoever assaulted her last didn't even take the time to pull her skirt back down her legs. Her face was bruised and she was unconscious. I saw needles on the nightstand, like they were keeping her drugged. I crossed to the bed and touched her cheek. My dad had taught us, both through his words and the way he treated Mama and Tay, to respect women. We might wild out and ho around, but my brothers and me would never do no sick, weak shit like this. Her chest was barely moving up and down. I pulled her skirt down. "It's okay, li'l mama. We gone get you some help," I whispered to her. I turned to Darius.

"Say, go get one of them niggas' phones. Make sure you keep your gloves on. After we get them packed up, I want you to call 911 and report this shit. Toss the phone. Hopefully, the others will have info." He nodded and moved quickly. My team handled them bitch ass niggas roughly as they loaded them in the black Lexus GX 460s my family used for grab and go operations. I sat there with one of Prince's towels pressed to my head, still mugging them sorry bitches. The crew would head back tonight and prep them niggas for us for tomorrow. Briar and I had a room, though, so I figured why not use it? I waited until everything was in order and took off. By the time I made it back to the hotel, I was bleeding less. Walking in with a bloody towel would draw attention, though, and I didn't want to take the main elevators, either. I strolled casually into the stairwell then ran up the six flights of stairs.

Briar took one look at me when I walked into the room and gasped. I didn't realize she had walked up on me as I turned to close the door until I felt her little hand smack me in the back.

I turned around to grill her. "Ay! What the hell wrong with you? Can't you see a nigga already injured?"

"I told you to be careful!" She popped me again, this time on my arm.

"For real, Briar Rose. Stop hitting me. You act like I tried to get shot!"

"You could've died, Tyrese! It's a head wound."

I tried to lighten her mood. "Girl, I got reflexes like The Flash," I said, smiling at her. My smile always got to chicks. She mugged me and mushed the unwounded side of my head. Briar was trying to look fierce, but in her Hello, Kitty pajamas, she just looked cute.

"You must've been moving slow today then, Mr. Flash. Sit down so I can look at this." Despite her attitude, she treated the graze gently. "It's a flesh wound, but head injuries bleed a lot. Were you the only casualty? You know next time you might not be so lucky!" she fussed after cleaning my wound and bandaging it.

I shrugged. "They had a girl there they messed up pretty bad. We called 911. As far as what might happen next time, that's the game, Shorty."

She mushed my head again. "How can you be so nonchalant about your life? Maybe it's time to leave the game!" I watched as she flounced over to the bed.

"First of all, ol' bossy ass girl, I'll leave the game when I'm ready. Secondly, you a little too happy with them hands. You better be glad my parents raised me right. But don't push your luck," I warned her as I headed for the shower. I started the water and began to strip. Standing there naked, I texted my brothers a brief description. Bones would give the full run down. There were a couple of knocks on the door and Briar pushed her way in.

"I brought you pain-" She blushed and whirled around to face the door. "Why you not in the shower yet? Oh, my God! I'm so sorry. I was just going to put some pills and water on the counter. I can't believe-"

"It's not a big deal," I told her. She tried to open the door, but I moved quickly to close it.

"There go them Flash like reflexes," I teased her.

She sighed. "You should've used them earlier. Stop playing and let me out."

"Did you like what you saw?" I asked as I grinded against her.

"Ty!"

"Yes…" I kissed one side of her neck. "…or no?" I kissed the other.

She turned to glare at me. "You are too much!"

"I told you that in the car." I grabbed her hand and dragged it down to my crotch so she could feel me on brick. Her eyes widened, but she slowly closed her hand around me and pulled once. Then she jumped like she'd been burned.

"I'm going to bed," she announced as I laughed at her scary ass.

"You coulda just said 'yes.'"

I took a quick shower before climbing into bed behind her. She tossed and turned until I reached over and smacked her on her round ass. She shrieked. "Be still, girl. I'm tired."

"Well…" she flipped over to look at me and took a deep breath like she had to build up her nerves. "I'm not. I'm horny." She let her hand trail across my bare chest.

"See, I knew you liked what you saw. Throwing hints with them Hello, Kitty pajamas. You want me to say hello to this kitty, don't you?" I cupped her between her legs and petted her. She moaned as she nodded. "You bring any toys with you?" I quizzed her, as I returned her touch, feeling her nipple harden beneath my palm.

"No. Should I have?" she asked in a whisper.

"Mm-hmm." I leaned in to kiss her, running my tongue along her lips as I squeezed her nipple.

She sighed and reached for me. I backed away. "You should've brought some toys if you wanted to get off, li'l mama. You not getting my goodies til you decide I'm not your side piece." I said.

Briar mugged me. "You cannot be serious?"

"I got standards, Dr. Rose."

"Ugh!" she screamed and flopped back over. I spooned her little mean ass and fell asleep in minutes.

Shamar

I couldn't believe Anton asked me out for brunch Saturday morning. I could tell he was really feeling me and I liked him, too. It was a pretty, warm day, so I put on a little pink sundress with an empire waist that gave me room for my baby. Once my morning sickness stage passed, I realized that I was enjoying my pregnancy. Reading about the development of the little person who was busy growing inside me fascinated me. Cyn and Devyn swore I had a glow, and even my problems with Tremell couldn't keep me down for long. I hopped into my car and watched as Ced prepared to follow me. Oh, well, he could report back to Tremell all he wanted. He was probably posted up with Katerah's tramp ass, anyway. I wish he would try to start some shit!

Anton and I met at The Egg and I. He was already there and greeted me at the door. I pushed my Yves St. Laurent shades up on my head and accepted his hug and kiss on my cheek. He put a hand on my lower back and guided me to a table. I eagerly reached for the menu. I was starving. Of course, I *always* felt like I was starving now.

"What are you having?" I asked him.

He scanned the menu quickly. "I guess I'll be good and have the oatmeal. But I gotta have a blueberry pancake, too."

I just looked at him. I should probably be embarrassed for what I was about to do, but I wasn't. Our server, Alex, arrived to take our drink order.

"I'll give you another minute to look over the menu-" she began. I was already shaking my head. Hungry and impatient, I was ready to order.

"I think we both know what we want," I said. I let Anton order his little skimpy meal first.

"And you, ma'am?" Alex said turning to me.

"Let me get the two-egg breakfast. I want the eggs scrambled and I want extra bacon, extra potatoes, the French toast, a biscuit with gravy, and the fruit and yogurt," I rambled off, then smiled at her. Alex and Anton looked at me, looked at each other, then looked back at me.

"Will that be all?" Alex asked. Her voice was quiet like she was scared of my answer.

"Oh! Please add salsa and avocado on the side! This baby makes me hungry."

"I see," she muttered before disappearing.

"I have no idea where you put that food," Anton commented.

"Ha! Have you seen my ass and thighs?" I asked.

"Yes, and to God be the glory." He lifted his hands like he was praising. "Keep eating, Shay." We both laughed, then chatted for a few minutes about nothing in particular. Eventually, he reached across the table to take my hand. "I know you can tell that I really like spending time with you."

I cleared my throat. "Yeah. You're cool, too, Anton."

"Just cool?" He tilted his head as he questioned me.

I squeezed his hand. "You know I have a lot going on. I'm pregnant and I really do care about Tremell. You deserve better than being a rebound guy."

"Just keep spending time with me. I'm sure I can get past that status." He gave me a cocky grin and I couldn't help smiling back. Anton was a cutie.

"Speaking of spending time, you busy after this?" he asked, cutting into his pancake.

"Nope," I said. "What's up?"

"Wanna go to a basketball tournament? I have some friends playing and some of the teams are supposed to be really good."

I nodded. I actually loved basketball. Tavion used to play before he quit school and I'd made every game I could. "I'd like that. I bet it's the same one my brother mentioned he was playing in today." Before I could say anything else, Alex appeared with my buffet. I had to keep myself from clapping my hands in excitement. Anton just watched as I mixed the avocado and salsa into my eggs then crumbled the bacon on top of the mixture, before stirring it all up with the potatoes.

I looked at him, a little self-conscious. "I know it probably looks disgusting, but it's *soooo* good. I couldn't even stand the smell of eggs my first trimester and now I can't get enough of them. Them and avocados!" I was rambling as I mixed my food together. And then I took my first bite.

I moaned. He just shook his head in amazement.

TREMELL

aturday morning dawned bright and beautiful. Despite my issues with Shamar, I was in a good mood. Ced told me she was out with that dude Anton. I had to woo-sah about 50 times. I was really tryna respect what my mama said, but today was gone be her last day entertaining that little wannabe gangster. In the meantime, I was going to watch Tamir play in a basketball tournament this afternoon. And then, tonight, I got to have my favorite kind of fun. Ty's mission had been successful. All I wanted was Prince's son, Stephen, but we got the added bonus of two of his chiefs. It was going to be a good night because I was going to get to act out some of my frustrations.

I hopped up out the bed to shower and fix breakfast. Tripp was meeting me at the gym and I knew we were going to lift heavy and go hard. I fixed oatmeal with peanut butter, turkey bacon, and four eggs—had to get my protein in. I grabbed my vitamins and water on the way out the door. My mama was headed out, too. I kissed her on top of the head, then picked her up and spun her around a little. She squealed and popped my arm. "Boy, behave," she said, but she was smiling.

"Love you, Drea!"

Mama mugged me. "Tremell Nicholas Kinsey, you done lost your mind. You know I don't play that first name mess," she scolded gently.

I kissed her again. "Yes, *mi jefita*." I called her that, because that's exactly what she was—the little boss of our family. She shooed me away as her driver pulled up.

"Ma, be careful," I said seriously. By now, Prince probably knew we had his son. If that nigga came for my mama...

She blew me a kiss. "Always, baby. I'm not new to this; I'm true to this." I laughed at her corny self then jumped into my new Range. I promised myself not to piss Shamar off while driving this one—and made my way to the gym. For once, my brother beat me there. He talked shit about it, too, til I threatened to drop weights on his throat while spotting him.

"I'm telling Mama," he grumbled.

I grilled him. "Y'all some snitches, man." Tripp laughed and started loading weights on the bar.

We cooled down at the end of the workout by walking on treadmills. "You and Cyn good?"

He smiled. "Yeah. She just crazy as hell. But my baby learning new words and math facts every day and she got into the kindergarten we wanted. I want her to start taking language classes—she at a good age."

I stopped for a moment and almost fell off the treadmill as I stared at him. Math facts? Language classes?

"What?" Tripp asked defensively. "Wait til Shamar has the baby. I'm praying it's a girl so I can watch you nut up more often."

I shook my head. "Don't wish that shit on me. I ain't turning into your soft ass."

For the next few minutes, he teased me about how he couldn't wait on his second niece, how they were gon spoil her and make her a nightmare for me. I finally put in my earbuds until our thirty minutes were up. We would meet up at the tournament in a little while, but I had to get fresh.

I went back home and showered. Since it was a basketball tourney, I slipped on some black and gold Jordan shorts, a black t-shirt, and my black and gold 12s. I turned my black, fitted hat to the side a little and sprayed on some Creed. A nigga knew he looked good. And y'all know I can't be all simple. I slipped on the Audemars Piguet watch that had been a gift from my mama just before I went in. She swore she'd keep time on it til I got out. Tay was standing at the foot of the stairs texting when I jogged down.

"You ain't fly," she teased me. I kissed her forehead. I was extra in my feelings about my baby sister since that planned hit.

"You going to the tournament?" I asked.

She shrugged. "I'on know. Prolly."

Grabbing her in a hug, I told her, "Stay with your detail, Tamar Noelle."

Tay brushed me off. "I'm sick of all this babysitting. My last name is Kinsey, too. I'm packing just like y'all. I'm a grown-" She stopped as I grilled her.

"Just do what I said." She rolled her eyes and stomped up the stairs in a huff. I shook my head and rolled out.

I'm a punctual type of nigga. No CPT for me. But even though I arrived well ahead of the first tip-off time, that bitch was already packed and the DJ had it jumping. Mir's team was playing the first game and he was on the court warming up. I strolled out there to talk to him while he was shooting.

"You ready?"

He looked at me like, "Nigga, what type of question is that?" but all he said was, "It's ball. I stay ready to keep from getting ready." He backed up his sentence with a perfect three-point-shot. Tripp joined us a few minutes later. He dapped us up.

"Late ass," Mir mumbled.

Tripp shrugged. "Not my fault my girl wanted a quickie," he said smugly, waving at Cyn and Naa in the stands. The baby waved back. Cyn, being Cyn, screwed up her pretty face and flipped him off before blowing a kiss.

"Mine did, too, nigga. I still got here early," Mir shot back.

I frowned. "Ol' minute man ass. Bet she didn't even get hers."

"Yo, big bro, I ain't you!" We continued like that for a few seconds. Suddenly, Tripp threw up his hand.

"Wait, nigga, wait!" He pointed at Mir. "Who the hell is yo girl? Last I heard, Chantal wasn't even speaking to your dog ass." Tamir grinned big and made another shot. Tripp and I looked at each other.

"Chantal let you smash? Nigga-"

Mir grilled him. "Watch your mouth, Tristan. That's my baby mama. I don't smash her." He grinned again. "I make love to her with these long strokes," he said, imitating his technique right on the middle of the court.

"Nobody wanna hear that shit, nasty boy," I said. "Maybe y'all lame asses can get married and stop showing out."

His face got serious again. "Nah, she ain't trusting me like that yet. But she will. She coming with the baby in a little while. Make sure she sits with y'all. Hate to have to kill one of these bitch ass niggas behind my ladies." I nodded and wished him luck.

"Baby bro don't need that. I got skills. Plus, Tavi supposed to be on my team. That nigga cold with it, but he ain't here yet. NiNi probably having issues. I know he'll be glad when she drops that load."

Tripp and I crossed the gym to sit with Cyn and Naa. Cyn mugged me.

"I'ma tell you right now if yo little bitch try to come sit with us, I'm beating her ass," she popped off.

Tripp rolled his eyes. "Don't start, Cyn Claire."

I mugged her back. "How you doing, Cyn? Good to see you, too. And I ain't got no little bitch."

"You right. The bitch ain't little," she muttered. I ignored her and turned my attention to Cynaa. It had taken her a minute to warm up to me—Shamar claimed cuz I always looked mean as hell—but she spent so much time with me and Mouse til she now hugged me and talked me to death.

The game was getting ready to start when Chantal walked in with Noah on her hip. Even though he was supposed to be doing the pre-game drills, Mir stopped, got her attention, and pointed to us. That nigga had it bad. She pursed her lips at him, but walked over to where we were. I reached for Noah so she could climb the bleachers and settle next to Cyn.

Mir was definitely one of the stars of the game. Nigga made some sick shots that had me and Tripp talking cash shit in the stands. He'd always been talented enough to pursue basketball on a higher level, but his heart wasn't in it. Mir brought the first quarter to an end with a beautiful ass dunk that had me and Tripp on our feet, yelling and dapping niggas around us.

I laughed and said, "That nigga cold!" Suddenly, while I was talking to my brother, a hush fell over the crowd. Tripp noticed it at the same time. "Fuck, fuck, fuck!" he said quietly under his breath.

I looked up to see what the hell had everybody's attention. My eyes landed on Anton and Shamar walking into the gym. *What the fuck?* Everything Mama said went out the window. I was tired of playing with her disrespectful ass. Then she had the nerve to be looking gorgeous for him. She was pretty in pink, her skin glowed, and my baby had her little stomach sitting up. She was cheesing hard at something he was saying. I turned to Tripp and said, "Call Dimitri and tell him where he can pick up his brother's body.

"Man, hold up-" Tripp grabbed my shoulder but I jerked away.

"You bet not touch her," hollered Cyn.

I ignored both of them as I walked down the bleachers. As I started towards Shamar and Anton, I could see the uncertainty in Shamar's face. She looked like she wanted to turn around. Anton just kinda smirked. I almost felt bad that they didn't have enough protective instinct to be scared.

To be terrified.

Because there was definitely about to be bloodshed. What the fuck was wrong with her? Did she truly think I was some punk ass, bitch nigga? That I would allow her to calmly step into my hood with this blond motherfucker and it not be shit?

As I made it to stand in front of them, I noticed my brothers, waiting to see if I wanted them to come stand with me. They must've looked at my eyes and saw the darkness. In that moment, I heard somebody say, "That nigga look crazy as hell." *Absolutely correct*, I thought. I didn't need my brothers. I didn't need any damned body, because I could fuck up this entire complex. Consumed by my rage, I looked directly at Shamar and asked the question boiling in my head.

"Have you lost your fuckin' mind?"

She had the nerve to raise her chin and look me in my eyes. "Look, Tremell, we don't want any problems. Just like you, I'm here to see my brother play."

While not touching her, I walked her ass backwards until she was up against the wall and said louder, "Have you LOST your fuckin' mind?!? You must want problems coming up in here with this bitch ass white boy!"

Suddenly, from the corner of my eye, I noticed Anton reach his hand out, as if to touch me. "Hey, leave her-"

That was all I remembered. I hit him so hard, my hand felt as if it was broken from the power of the punch. He lunged at me, swinging and hitting me squarely in the face. Nigga had good hands on him, but I only half-registered the punch. I was too enraged to really feel it. I was finna dead this nigga. I wanted to stomp him until he was nothing but a fucking blood stain.

I felt like we were fighting in a vacuum. As if there were not a gym full of spectators watching as we went blow for blow. I couldn't sec or hear shit except my target. Suddenly, I noticed he was staggering from the weight of my last blow and I pounced on the opportunity to land three quick jabs and an uppercut. As he fell to his knees, I kicked him with enough force to send him flat on his back. I stomped him with the full force of my weight.

Abruptly, I felt hands pulling me back. Both of my brothers were attempting to drag me off him and Tavion had finally showed up and was in the mix, too. Them niggas struggled with me because I wanted to finish what I started. I wanted Anton dead. As my brothers finally got me locked down, I noticed Dimitri had arrived. He nodded to his team to pick Anton up, then he stared into my eyes. An unspoken agreement passed between us. He was pissed off but he knew I could have killed his brother. His young ass made a choice to come to *my* territory with *my* damned pregnant girl. He was lucky that all he got was his ass handed to him. I gave a slight nod.

"Get your damn hands off me!" I yelled at Mir, Tripp, and Tavi.

"Chill nigga, you ain't finna beat our asses like that," Mir snapped, but they backed up off me. Swear I hated that little dude and his mouth sometimes. I turned to locate Shamar. I saw her crying softly in Cyn's arms.

"What in the fuck are you crying for? Isn't this what the fuck you wanted? Didn't I tell you to sit YOUR FUCKIN' ASS down?"

"I got mad respect for you, Tre, but you not finna keep talking to my sister like that. You gon' stress her and the baby," Tavion said, grilling me.

I almost stole on his little ass, too, but I knew he was right.

She finally looked at me, her eyes red-rimmed, her mouth trembling. I shook my head and said, "Go get in the motherfucking car, Shamar."

I saw terror in her eyes. That shifted my mood like nothing else. I mean, I thought I wanted her to be scared of what I might do to someone else, but never to her. She was actually shaking.

"Leave her alone, Tre," Cyn said.

"Cyn Claire." Tripp's voice had none of its usual humor toward her smart-ass mouth. Cyn swallowed, mugged me, but didn't say anything else.

Shamar looked up at me again. She had tears in her eyes but she was no longer letting them fall. "I hear all these things about you… about what you're capable of. But I never thought I'd see it. You almost killed my friend just because we were here together. How do I know what you'll do to me?"

That shit gutted me. Like, I literally had to take a step back. Shorty hurt me with that one; I couldn't even play it off.

"I told you when I first met you what I do, how I solve problems. So what you expect? I'm Tremell Nicholas Kinsey. I will beat a nigga's ass, without a second thought, and destroy anyone who stands in the way of me getting and keeping what's mine. Cuz see, that's a problem to me. And you? *You. Are. Mine.*"

She wasn't feeling me, even after I tried to explain. Suddenly, my mama's warning and her words came back to me.

"Mir?"

"Wazzam, bro?"

"Can you get the DJ's microphone for me?" He frowned, but did what I asked.

After making sure it was on, I started talking. "All y'all sit your asses down. You got the show you came for. And I got some shit to say." I cleared my throat as the crowd, of course, obeyed me. I was more uncomfortable than I had ever been in my life. But as I looked at my Mouse, I knew I had to do something different or I was gone lose her. "Look at me," I ordered her. She turned her head. "Shamar... please?" Shit, I didn't even know I knew how to pronounce that last word. Shamar sighed and finally grilled me.

"Ima say this publicly because I've done so much other shit publicly and I wanna set the record straight. I... um... I care a lot about you." *Weak. Try harder, Tre,* I told myself. "That shit you just said, like I would physically hurt you, Ma, that's an impossibility. It ain't a lot of shit in the world that makes a nigga like me happy. But seeing you happy makes me happy. You... make me happy. Umm.... ain't nobody on this earth ever made me feel like you. I know you my sunshine and soft. But it's more than that. You like," I cleared my throat again. The sound was loud because the gym was silent. "You my everything. Seeing you with someone else, I ain't gone never be able to deal with that, Shorty. I just ain't built that way. I'm sorry for hurting you, though. I guess... I guess what I'm saying is, I love you, Mouse." Swear the whole gym gasped. Shamar's jaw dropped. Even Cyn was back to liking me right then—she gave me a thumbs up. "I ain't never said that shit to no bitch before—I mean you ain't a bitch," I said hurriedly when she started to mug me. "I just... I need one more chance, Mouse."

She looked at me for a long minute. If this girl had me up in here embarrassing myself... I focused on what my mama said, though, about it being ok to be vulnerable with somebody you love. Finally, she stepped toward me and smiled. She grabbed my face and I leaned down to kiss the hell out of her. The gym broke out in applause and catcalls. I quickly spoke into the mike again. "Yo, if I catch anybody talking about this mushy shit again, I'ma body yo ass." The handclapping stopped. Shamar shook her head at me. I just kissed her again.

"Get a damned room. We tryna play ball," Tavion muttered. I flipped him off.

Shamar pulled back long enough to whisper, "I love you, too."

I probably should've realized when Cyn started looking mean as hell who was approaching. Katerah walked up to us with tears in her eyes. "So that's how it is? You gone humiliate me like this?" She hissed. I mushed her head.

"Girl, if you don't go away. You knew the deal—I ain't even touch you, ma."

She turned to glare at Shamar. "Don't get too happy. He'll be back shortly."

"Ok, I done had enough of this bitch," said Shamar. Before I could stop her, she slapped the hell out of Katerah, then grabbed her hair and crashed her first into Katerah's temple.

"No, Shay, we got this!" Chantal said. Already, she was trying to get between them. All of us saw that Katerah's fists were aiming for Shamar's belly.

I yoked that bitch up by her throat and leaned into her face. The color left her face. "If you *ever* try to hurt my seed, I will make you watch as I kill everybody in your trifling family." I threw her away from me. She landed on her ass and slid across the floor. I turned to Shamar.

"How you gone put my baby at risk like that?" I asked grilling her.

"I'm sick of you and that bitch. You got her thinking-"

I wasn't doing this shit here. "Let's go!"

"No!"

"GO GET IN THE MUTHERFUCKING CAR, SHAMAR!" I bellowed.

She tilted her head high, turned, and started towards the door. "I don't even know what the fuck you driving," she snapped.

"Yo little ass betta figure it out!" With a nod to my brothers, I started behind her. Today already had me ready to go off on one. But a little voice was telling me, my biggest fight was yet to come, and it was going to be an emotional battle once we made it home.

Chantal

Mir's sweaty ass was walking beside me and Noah. He was laughing, happy because they'd won the championship, and talking shit to Tripp who was walking close by with his family. My baby's daddy was so beautiful to me. I looked at him for a minute, trying to get every detail in my memory--his sparkling eyes, the droplets of sweat, his braided dreads, the sunlight shining on him, his perfect smile. I knew I was going to have to sketch and possibly paint him like this.

"*Qu'est-ce qui ne va pas?*" he said, asking me what was wrong. "Why you looking at me like that?"

I just smiled at him. "Nothing. I just love you," I told him truthfully. He tried to wrap an arm around me and I ran a few steps ahead. "Sorry, mon coeur, you stink."

Tripp laughed. "That don't sound like no unconditional love to me, Chan." I stuck out my tongue at him.

"Tristan, mind your business," Cyn said, mimicking what he always told her. We all laughed--even the detail (everybody knew Cyn's personality by now)--as we made our way to the parking lot. Mir walked me to my car. I leaned my back against the door and faced him.

"I love y'all," he said, kissing our baby, then me.

"We love your funky ass, too," I teased.

He leaned in to kiss me deeper, but jerked back when we heard someone call his name. My eyes followed his. That bitch

Daria was approaching us with two of her friends. She had a baby boy in her arms. My face dropped immediately.

Mir grilled her. "Don't bring your ignorant ass here with this shit," he said.

She came closer to my car. I mugged her. Behind us, I heard Cyn say, "Baby, hold my earrings. These my good hoops." I struggled not to laugh. I was starting to love that crazy chick. "Didn't I beat your ass once for approaching us like you ain't got good sense?" I asked.

"Yeah, but she got her hittas with her today," one of the busted up bitches she had with her said. "Try it today, see what happens, ol' foreign ho!" she threatened. I handed Noah to her daddy, but before I could respond, Cyn was beside me talking.

"My girl might be foreign, but you know what's all-American? This blunt force trauma I'll put upside your head if you bitches think you gone jump her. Please get froggy. *Please*!"

"Ain't nobody jumping her unless they wanna end up floating in one of these damned bayous," Mir said.

Daria sighed. "Look, I didn't come for no mess. I came because it's time you acknowledge your son."

Tripp laughed around the toothpick he was chewing. "Talking about that glow-in-the-dark baby you named after a white man? You scandalous!"

If looks could kill, Daria would've had us burying Tripp right then. "Don't talk about my baby. He's innocent. And after Mir rejected us because of this-" she looked me up and down.

I put a hand on my hip and dared her.

She cleared her throat. "Because of Chantal, I had to make sure my baby would be taken care of and I knew Robert was a good man."

"Here's a thought. Instead of depending on a man, you could

get an education and a job. That way, all you need a man to do for your child is his part. You wouldn't have to be as desperate as you sound right now," I schooled the bitch.

"Easy for you to say, when your baby daddy got you set up lavish," she spat at me.

"Look, bitch-" Mir waved his hand, cutting me off.

"Daria, that baby don't look nothing like me. Look at Noah. There's no doubt," he said.

"I have strong genes. I didn't lay back and get run over." She grilled me again.

I was gone have to whoop her ass again. That's all it came down to.

"It's not fair to Bobby-" Daria started.

"Bobby? Unless his last name 'Brown,' you setting him up for an ass whooping in the hood." Tripp cracked. He and Cyn were making it damned near impossible for me to keep a straight face.

Daria rolled her eyes. "Tripp, why don't you shut up, damn! Anyway, look how you cuddling your little girl. Bo-" she cut her eyes at Tripp. "My baby deserves that, too. He deserves to have you spend time-"

"And money," Cyn mumbled sarcastically.

"-with him. It's not fair. He's your family, too." This bitch actually had tears in her eyes.

Tripp clapped his hands. "Damn, girl! You a ho *and* an actress? Look at your multitalented ass!" Daria was ready to erupt.

"Give us a test," I said. "Let DNA speak. If he's Noah's brother, y'all go from there."

She swallowed as Tamir nodded.

"That shit struck fear in yo heart, huh, ho?" Cyn laughed.

"Fine," Daria said, but she sounded unsure.

"We'll set it up. Now you and the rest of yo broke down crew can get on," Mir said, waving at them. With one final sneer, Daria stomped off.

Tripp and Cyn said their goodbyes to us in a flurry of hugs and kisses and I stole some sweet sugar from Cynaa as she slept in Tripp's arms. I was quiet as I started my car and reached for my baby to strap her in.

"Baby-" Mir started.

"It shouldn't even be a possibility, Tamir. I don't wanna talk right now."

He spun me around. "We ain't going backwards. Let's just find out and go from there?"

"Go where? If that baby is yours, he absolutely should be in your life and I want Noah to know her project twin. But you and I can't go anywhere--I could love your child; he's half you. But I can't live the next 18 years with Daria. I'll end up in jail."

I slid into the driver's seat and shut the door.

"DuBois!"

I pulled off.

Tristan

I guess one thing you can never say about my family is that we boring. Tre surprised me so much at the gym that I was still wondering if he had been cloned. The right woman could make you feel like that, though. I still couldn't wait to tell Ty. He was gone blues Tre's ass. Then again, his unknown doctor had him all in his feelings. Nigga might start crying. And I don't know how shit was gone work out with Mir and Chantal.

As usual, me, Mir, Tavi, Bones, Roy, and Case were at the warehouse. Tre was waiting for Ty before he came. For some reason, that nigga had spent some extra time in the metroplex. Prolly fucking the whole Dallas Cowboys Cheerleaders' line up. I shook my head. One day he was tired of playing games, the next, he was singing that line from an old Young Money song: *I wish I could fuck every girl in the world.*

I snapped back to the present. I wonder what Tre had in store for these niggas. Stephen Prince was bound to a chair, but his two chiefs were literally hanging by chains. One of them was face down with chains from his wrists and ankles anchoring him. The other was currently hanging upside down although Bones shifted him every once in a while so the rush of blood didn't destroy his brain before Tre got there. As sloppy as their technique was that led to them getting caught, they were trying to be decent soldiers now. They were absolutely silent, even though we'd done some initial prodding and poking and Roy had calmly quizzed them.

Mir moved to stand in front of Stephen Prince. Roy had been trying to ask him about the hit on Tay, but the nigga just kept smirking. "Stephen," Mir said. "Let me tell you a story."

Shit, this nigga was getting more like Tre's psychotic ass everyday. I shook my head.

Prince sneered. "I ain't got time for no bitch ass-" Mir whipped him upside the head with his gun. Weak ass nigga passed out.

"Damn, Mir. You supposed to knock him out *after* the story. Now we gotta wait to hear it!" Bones complained.

"Sorry!"

"Tre got you as fucked up as he is with them stories," Case told Bones.

Bones shrugged. "Makes the shit more interesting."

Tre and Ty walked in. Tre looked at Prince. "What happened to this nigga?" he asked.

I winked at Mir. "Your baby bro got mad because Prince didn't want to listen to his story."

Tre looked genuinely hurt. "Mir! You know stories are *my* thing."

"Sorry, nigga, damn." The he turned to me. "Snitches get stitches," he hissed. I smiled at him.

Tre slapped Prince a few times. "Hey! Wake your ass up, punk ass nigga. Who put a hit on my sister?" Prince grilled him.

"Obviously you know who or we wouldn't be here. Come on, now. Rumors have it that the Kinseys are brilliant. You're disappointing me, Tre."

Tre returned his grill. "I'ma disappoint you a lot in the next few days, trust. What I wanna know right now is, who had the idea and who specifically ordered it?"

Prince just hunched up his shoulders.

"You know, if I could find your scary, bitch ass daddy, I'd ask him. But that pussy is hiding. So here's what we gone do. Instead of giving you back to him, dead all at once, Ima make a generous offer. I'm just gon send a piece of you to him everyday until he shows his face. And just to emphasize how generous I am, Ima let you choose the parts you need least. That's assuming your pops cares enough about you to come collect what's left. I kinda doubt his cowardly ass."

Prince stared at him in disbelief. "Did you take your meds this morning, Tre? You're a lunatic! I'm not finna volunteer no body parts of mine."

Tre stroked his beard and ignored Prince. "What you think? A pinkie? A little toe? The outside of your ear?"

"Man, *fuck you*. Yeah, we coming for your sister cuz we coming for your *heart*. All the problems y'all done caused for us--ain't nothing off limits anymore. The Kinseys are going down and we're going to piss on you."

All of us grilled his ass then. I moved forward, ready to finish what Mir started. But then, Tre's crazy ass started doing a slow clap. "Bravo, Stephen, Bra-fucking-vo. Definitely Golden Globe worthy. Did you practice that?" He leaned down into Prince's face. "Which part? Answer my question."

Stephen Prince made the biggest mistake of his life.

He spit in my brother's face. Everyone in the room looked at each other. Tre stood up and smiled. "Such a violent reaction! It's my turn to be disappointed in you. I'ma go wash this off. Wait right there for me, Stephen."

While Tre was in the bathroom, I ain't gone lie—I think we all felt a little nervous. That nigga just gave off that vibe. He finally reappeared and crossed to his tables. As he decided what he wanted, this nigga was humming. I watched as he put on gloves and covered himself in the thick plastic that already covered the floor. Tre walked over to Prince with a pair of something—I couldn't tell if that shit was pliers or scissors.

"I asked you what you wanted to remove first and you spit on me. I thought maybe you were refusing to answer. And then I remembered that you asked me to illustrate my brilliance. I realized then that you wanted me to figure out what you meant by spitting on me. Very clever, Stephen, but I solved the riddle." That nigga paused for dramatic effect. I swear I was holding my breath—I think everyone was. "Obviously, you want me to start with your tongue." He stunned Prince with a blow to his head then calmly clipped off his tongue. Even I had to close my eyes for a minute as blood spurted. Tre sat it on the table beside Prince.

"Y'all don't let me misplace that," he said, like he was talking about keys or some shit.

Bones started fussing. "How he gone talk now, Tre?"

"Bitch betta start writing," Tre said, his tone nonchalant. "Let's talk to our other guests."

As Tre moved toward his hanging targets, the one who was hanging by all fours started shaking his head. Obviously what he had seen spooked him. He spoke for the first time.

"I... I wanna talk to the old man. I got some stuff to say, but I wanna talk to the old man first," he said.

Tre looked at me. "What you think?" I just shrugged.

"I think it can't hurt," Ty said.

Roy nodded. "Let me work," he said. We stepped back.

"Shane, right?" Roy said. The man nodded. "What you got for me, Shane?"

The dude really didn't have much new info. Alonzo was in the background, he said, letting Stephen have more and more control. Stephen had ordered the hit on our middle-class trap and had the idea to put a price on Tay's head. His father gave him permission. He didn't know where Alonzo was hiding and we already knew the international hideaways the older Prince owned that Shane mentioned. He had no idea why the Princes' started with us, beyond greed.

"Look, can I cut y'all a deal now? I cooperated."

"Let me tell you a story, Shane," Mir and Tre said at the same time.

Ty rolled his eyes.

"What is it with your families and stories?" Shane asked with a nervous smile.

Tre was mean mugging Mir. "You gon let me do my thing, or you gon take over my job, Youngsta?" Mir rolled his eyes but nodded once.

"Thanks. Now, Shane, once upon a time, there was a little boy. He never knew who his daddy was. His mama loved him to death and did everything for him. He didn't have much time to worry about his deadbeat sperm donor. But one day, as a young man, he just had to know. So he did some research. Know what he found out, Shane?"

Shane shook his head slowly. Tre looked at him hard.

"You don't even wanna guess? Make the story interactive?" He asked.

The terrified chief licked his dry lips. "Maybe, he found out that-"

Tre waved his hand, cutting off the man's timid response. "Ain't nobody got time to hear what you think. That his beautiful mama had been raped. That's why she never told him about his father. He was a child of rape. He vowed he would NEVER hurt a woman like that. He found it one of the most disgusting, disturbing acts that could happen. He passed those ideas on to his four sons. They find it as just as terrible as their father. You know who those brothers are?"

He shook his head.

"Oh, I think you do," Tre said as the four of us raised our hands. The stupid fucker finally realized what was up.

"Now," Tre continued, walking to his table. "My brother Ty found a young woman assaulted in a house with you. He was pissed off."

Shane started shaking his head rapidly. "I had nothing to do with that. I swear to God. Please listen to me. I didn't touch that-"

"Shut up and man up!" Ty snapped.

Tre nodded. "I'on believe you, Shane. Thing is, even if you didn't touch her yourself, you didn't stop it. Just like you didn't try to do anything about the hit on my sister. You sit back while women are raped and drugged and murdered. And that makes you less than a man." Tre pulled out a long ass knife with some kind of hook at the end. He walked back to Shane and stood near his chest.

"Tre. Please listen," that nigga begged.

Tre turned his head to the side. "Listen? Did you listen to that girl? Did she have tears in her eyes, too? Looking up at least three big ass niggas about to hurt her?"

"I swear-"

But Tre was tired of excuses. "Yo, wake that other nigga up," he told Bones. Bones slapped the shit outta dude and he and Tavi propped him up. He stabbed the knife into Shane's abdomen and pulled it across as the nigga screamed.

We found out what the hook was for. Tre pulled and that nigga's guts fell out. Case, true to style, started to throw up. Tre smiled. "Whooooo! I needed that. Been wanting to do that to some piece of shit."

"Yo, Tre, that nigga ain't dead," Ty said as Shane moaned and cried. He looked like he wanted to pass out.

"It might take a few hours," my big brother explained.

The other chief started shaking his head. "Hey, yo. Yo, Mr. Kinsey, I know-" Tre whirled on him.

"Ain't nobody tell you it's rude to talk outta turn? You tryna steal your patna's shine? What kinda friend are you?"

"Just listen. I just want you to off me quick. I'll tell you what I know about how they planning the next hit on you."

"Talk to Roy," I said. "We might be able to accommodate your request." Tre turned to me.

"You never let me have any fun!"

"I gotta go," Tavi said suddenly. "We don't bring phones in here and Ni-Ni bout to pop any day. I gotta check in."

"I'd dap you up, but-" Tre began.

Tavi turned up his nose. "I'll pass."

Shamar

When we got home from the basketball tourney, Tremell and I were pretty quiet. He sat on my couch and watched a Law & Order *marathon* while I made sandwiches and soup and straightened up. I pulled out tray tables and served both of us. He finally looked at me.

"Thanks, Mouse." I nodded and we ate in silence for a minute. I had to break the quiet.

"Tremell, can we talk?" I don't know why I felt so nervous saying. He seemed to think about it for a little while. I watched as he moved back his little table and stood up. Then he moved mine from in front of me. Tremell pulled up by my hands.

"Tremell?"

He shook his head. "Talk later. I been missing you," he said, kissing me. I liked his idea even better. But wait…

"You told Katerah you didn't touch her-"

"I ain't fucked that girl since before I went to jail."

I gave him the side-eye. He shrugged. "She followed me home the night of the party. I let her suck me off, nutted on her face, and sent her on her way." I was pissed off but I wanted his honesty. Before I could object, Tremell picked me up and carried me into the bedroom. My arms went around his neck as I kissed him back. He set me down long enough to yank the comforter off. Before I knew it, we were both in our underwear. Just seeing his monster ass print had me soaking my panties. Suddenly, I had an idea.

"You trust me?" I asked him.

He raised an eyebrow. "What you talking about?"

"I wanted to try some things I heard about before you went off the deep end on me," I explained, jumping up. I ran into the kitchen as he was calling my name, demanding to know what I was doing. Grabbing a fruit roll-up, chocolate syrup, and a new feather duster, I ran back to my room.

"Ah, shit," he said approvingly. "I trust the hell out you, Bae." I smiled at him as I set the items on the night stand. Then, I went to dig through my dresser, finding four scarves. Tremell's face started to change. He looked like he was about to say, "Fuck all this," by the time I came back from the bathroom with some wet wipes.

"You gotta trust me all the way," I coaxed. I stood beside the bed. Tremell looked at the scarves, looked at the nightstand, looked at me. I pouted my lips to emphasize how full they were. He looked back at the nightstand and nodded hesitantly. I clapped my hands.

"Take off your underwear," I instructed. Slowly, he slid out of his boxer briefs. "Okay. Now spread out your arms and legs." Again, he moved slowly.

"Aye, Shamar, you bet not be about to do no crazy shit!"

I just smiled as I tied his arms and then his legs to my bedposts. When I was sure he was secure—I mean, I knew he could break free if he wanted to, but I didn't plan on him wanting to—I grabbed the chocolate syrup and fruit roll-up. I'd gotten this idea from a meme. Once Cyn and Devyn explained what the fruit roll-up was for, I was intrigued. I carefully drizzled chocolate syrup on the sides of his dick. Tremell sucked in his breath as I started to lick the sticky confection off. I worked each side with slow curls of my tongue, making my way to his tip.

195

"Damn, Mouse. What you been watching, Baby?" I smiled up at him and then sucked just the tip of him into my mouth. Little by little I eased down as far as I could. I couldn't claim to be a deep throat expert, but between my hand and my mouth and the way my man was moving restlessly beneath me, I think I was doing all right. My head bobbed up and down and I watched as he pulled on the restraints

"Uh-uh," I told him. "Don't be naughty." He stopped twisting his arms but gave me a warning look.

"If you don't slow down, Ma, I'ma bust," he said.

I slid my mouth down him one more time, making sure he was good and sticky and wet. Then, I released him and reached for the candy. I wrapped it around his dick. "What you know about that, Shorty?" he teased me.

"Enough, Daddy. And it's strawberry. My favorite. I'ma suck this til it's all gone."

I proceeded to do just what I said, enjoying the delicious strawberry and chocolate mix and the hint of saltiness that I could taste in his pre-cum. I was a perfectionist so I liked to be good at everything I do. This was no different and soon, I had the toughest gangsta in Houston speaking in tongues, encouraging me to suck harder, and telling me that this was just one more thing he loved about me. I loved being in control of his pleasure. He didn't even realize when I reached over to grab the duster. I swirled it over his balls as I pulled on him with my mouth. Tremell almost choked me as he thrust to the back of my throat. I popped him on the thigh.

"I'm bout to come, baby," he hissed. I kept teasing his balls and sucking him off. He was fucking my mouth in earnest, barely controlling himself. Suddenly, he tried to buck me off him, but I wouldn't let go. He'd never come in my mouth. This time, I

wanted him to. "Mouse, you-" I increased my suction a little. He broke one of the scarves on his wrists, grabbed my hair, and groaned as he fed me his seed. It slid down my throat easily and I did my best to suck him dry. When he finished, I swear that nigga couldn't move. I smiled as I knelt between his legs and grabbed the wipes. I cleaned him up quickly and he was hard again. Quickly, I straddled him and started to ease down onto his shaft. He stretched me as always, a little bit of pain, but a whole lot of pleasure.

"Tremell," I sighed.

Suddenly, my dream of our afternoon was tragically interrupted. I groaned, not wanting to give up my sleep. Tremell had tired my ass out. But Ced kept gently shaking my shoulder and calling my name. "Where's your phone, lady? Your brother been trying to call you. Ni-Ni is having the baby. Come on, I'll take you."

I jumped up and squealed, not caring that Ced could probably see all my pregnant ass in the t-shirt I wore. He just smiled and walked out. Wait til I saw Tremell. I knew that nigga probably took my phone when he went to work to make sure Anton didn't try to contact me. I dashed off a note to Tre after I brushed my teeth, washed my face, and pulled on some sweat pants.

"I'm ready!" I hollered as I ran out of my room. Ced shook his head at my loudness and just looked at me.

"Let's go," he said.

Tristan

I sped back home to Cyn and Naa. I knew they were probably already in bed, but my night wasn't complete until I set eyes on them, especially since that nigga claimed that the Princes' were planning another hit. He didn't know where it was, but he knew it was coming. I was ready to check on my family. I pulled up and jogged to the front door. I assumed Cyn had left the living room light on low for me, but she was up, sitting on the couch. There was no music on, no wine glass, no TV like usual when she waited up on me.

"What you sitting up in here like you crazy for?" I asked her as I walked over to her. It was then I noticed she'd been crying. I frowned and picked her up, then settled on the couch, holding her. "What is it, Cyn? Did somebody do something to you?"

My baby shook her head.

"Are you sick? Do you need to go-"

"No," she cut me off.

"Is it the baby?" She nodded and burst out into sobs. My heart dropped. "Where is she, Cyn? Where is Cynaa?" She just kept crying. I shook her shoulders and repeated my question. My shit was beating so fast I thought it was gon explode out my chest.

"She... she's in her b-b-bed," Cyn choked out. I frowned.

"Is she sick? Don't cry, baby. We can see about her." She just kept shaking her head. "Cyn Claire. I need you to calm down. I can't fix it unless you tell me what's wrong."

"Tristan! Oh my God. Aaron... Aaron is so crooked. He used his money... Tristan, he got somebody to declare me unfit. I didn't know he was planning this. Some judge awarded him c-c-custody. He's going to take my baby! Tristan, he's coming Monday and he's going to take my baby!"

This nigga. I'd been sparing his ass too long.

"Ain't nobody taking our baby nowhere. I put that on my life."

She looked at me. "How can we stop him? He has a court order!" I mugged her and out her out of my lap to stand up. My pride was kinda hurt. Obviously, she done forgot who I am. Before I could remind her, my work phone buzzed. I had to look at it. I was gon read the text quickly and get back to my family. But the words on the screen temporarily stopped my brain. Cyn noticed, stood up, and shook my arm.

"Tripp... Tristan, what's wrong?" she asked me. Sighing, I let her see the message.

I caught her as she collapsed.

TREMELL

I left the last chief alone to give him time to think after suspending him upright. I figured looking at Stephen's bloody mouth and watching his friend whine himself to death might jog his memory a little more. They were well-guarded and the cleanup crew would take care of that Shane nigga as soon as he took his last worthless breath.

My mind had already turned back to my baby girl. I was more than ready to get back to her and finish what we started. Pregnancy was making her horny and freaky and I was glad to indulge her. That shit she did earlier shocked me, but I swear that was the best nut I ever busted and then following it up by being in her hot, tight pussy… You can't blame me, can you?

I unlocked the door and started yelling her name. I didn't care about waking her up. I'd put her ass to sleep like I did before I left. Of course, she didn't respond, with her hard-sleeping ass. I opened her bedroom door and flipped on the light.

And almost went crazy when I didn't see her in the bed. I saw a piece of paper propped on her pillow and moved quickly to grab it. I smiled in relief as I read the message. After I couldn't get her or Ced, I called Tavion.

He answered after the first ring. "Sup?" he said.

"What hospital y'all at?"

"Huh?" he sounded confused. I hoped I didn't lose my fucking mind when Shamar went into labor.

"Tavi, where y'all having the baby?"

"Umm, the Woman's Hospital of Texas," he said, still sounding crazy.

I laughed. "Cool, nigga. I'll be there in a minute. You seen your sister?"

"Tre, are you fucked up from earlier?"

That shit made me frown. "What you talking about, nigga? I'ma come sit with y'all while Ni-Ni has the baby. Shamar left me a note that Ni-Ni was in labor and she and Ced were going to the hospital."

Silence. Then, "*Fuuuuuuuuuuck!*" I knew that wasn't good.

"What? What the fuck, Tavi?" I asked. "Nigga you betta tell me someth-"

"Ni-Ni right here with me. She not in labor and we ain't at no hospital. Somebody lied to get her out the house, Tre. We need to call everybody, start tracking her."

Tavi's words faded into the background. My girl, my love was missing. Nah, we were just about to start over. I still had to take her corny ass on some more dates. She-

"Tre?! Do you hear me? My sister is not with us. We gotta get-"

"Call my family," I said.

I'd take care of everything else.

At first, I was big mad that my brothers left me out of the interrogation tonight. And then, I got a message from Tavion. While they were out taking care of business, someone had taken Shay. I was worried about my friend and my growing niece or nephew. I was on my way to my parents' to meet up with my family. I expected to see one of my detail at my doorstep as I yanked it open. I didn't expect to see a shady figure dressed in black. He must have taken out my light. I reached for my gun, but he was faster. As he aimed his at my head, he extended his hand to take mine. He gestured with the gun, letting me know to walk in front of him.

Oh, shit. Looked like I was about to meet up with Shay sooner than I expected.

Tamir

"**W**hat?" DuBois said as I froze in the driver's seat. "Something's wrong with my twin," I said tightly. "Call her."

She obeyed quickly. Even before DuBois said, "She didn't answer," I knew. Suddenly, my phone rang. It was Austin. I slid my finger across the screen to answer it.

"Where my sister?" I asked abruptly.

"Mir... somebody knocked me over the head and-"

I growled. "Bitch, I'ma kill you. Slow!" My voice woke Noah. Sensing my stress, she began crying.

"The nigga left a card, Mir."

"What the fuck? Niggas going around snatching our women tonight and you worried about a card? Fuck a card!" I took a deep breath and acknowledged that might be the only clue we'd get. "Send all of us a picture of it. And you explain to my brothers and my parents what happened. Where the fuck is Max?"

"I-I-I guess he got clocked, too."

I hung up in that weak nigga face.

"What's going on?" DuBois asked, rocking Noah and calming her. I couldn't talk yet. I opened Austin's text as soon as my phone buzzed. That shit looked like some kind of Tarot card. I didn't have time to figure out no damned mystery.

"Fuck!"

DuBois stroked my arm. "Let me see, baby," she requested holding out her hand. I handed the phone over.

She looked at it for a minute. Her lips got tight.

"What? What is it, DuBois?"

"I think this is called the Prince of Death," she whispered.

Prince. These bastards were about to die.

JANE DOE

The beeping of the machinery around me was beginning to annoy me. I couldn't complain, though. My eyes wouldn't open and I couldn't talk. I hurt everywhere but it was a distant hurt--I knew they must be pumping me with medications.

It didn't stop the hurt inside my head. Stephen Prince was going to pay for kidnapping and repeatedly raping me. I swore that on my life.

My thoughts turned to the voice of my rescuer. All I knew from the way those bastards whispered after they got their asses kicked was that his last name was Kinsey. I was going to find him, too. Thank him. My hero. He'd saved me from addiction and death--they'd been injecting me with heroin, trying to turn me into someone they could pimp. He'd talked so softly to me, touched my face so gently. A man like that was one I could love.

Yes, I was going to find Mr. Kinsey. It was my last thought before I drifted off.

Made in the USA
Columbia, SC
22 December 2024

50446125R00117